PURRFECTLY HIDDEN

THE MYSTERIES OF MAX 16

NIC SAINT

PUSS IN PRINT PUBLICATIONS

PURRFECTLY HIDDEN

The Mysteries of Max 16

Copyright © 2019 by Nic Saint

Edited by Chereese Graves

www.nicsaint.com

Give feedback on the book at: info@nicsaint.com

facebook.com/nicsaintauthor
@nicsaintauthor

First Edition

Printed in the U.S.A

PROLOGUE

*M*arge loved these quiet mornings when she had the house all to herself. Tex and Vesta were at the office, and so were Odelia and Chase, and the cats were probably next door having a quiet nap, or out in the backyard wistfully gazing at the flock of birds occupying the big cherry tree. It was a gorgeous morning, and she enjoyed it to the fullest. She'd vacuumed upstairs and downstairs, had put in a load of laundry and was busy in the kitchen, humming along with Dua Lipa's latest hit blasting from the speakers, when suddenly the kitchen tap sputtered and hissed, then gurgled up a small trickle of brown water and promptly died on her.

"Dang it," she muttered as she tried the tap again, with the same result. She stared at the recalcitrant thing for a moment, hands on hips, willing it to work by the sheer force of her willpower, but faucets are tough opponents, and it decided to stay dead instead.

She heaved a deep sigh and called her husband.

"Hey, hon," said Tex as he picked up. "I'm with a patient right now. Can I call you back?"

"It's the kitchen faucet. It's broken."

"Broken, huh? Okay if I take a look at it tonight?"

"Yeah, fine," she said and disconnected. She thought for a moment, then went into the laundry room. It had been conspicuously quiet in there, and she now saw that the machine had stopped mid cycle. And when she opened the tap next to the washer, it was as dead as the one in the kitchen.

Ugh.

She returned to the kitchen and stood thinking for a moment, wondering whether to wait for Tex, but then her eye caught the pet flap Tex had installed in the kitchen door, the one that had cost him a week to put in place and for which he'd needed the help of her brother and Chase to finish, and she picked up her phone again and called her mom.

"I'm busy," said that sprightly old lady. "What do you want?"

"I've got a problem with my plumbing," she said.

"Ask Tex. He's the expert. And wear adult diapers."

"Not my plumbing, ma. The plumbing of the house."

"In that case diapers won't do you any good. And nor will Tex."

"You don't think Tex will be able to fix it?"

"Honey, that husband of yours can't even change a light-bulb without taking down the entire grid. Why don't you call Gwayn Partington? He's a licensed plumber."

"And an expensive one. What about Alec?"

"Forget about it. He's in your husband's league."

"Chase?"

Mom was quiet for a moment. She might not be a great fan of Tex or even her own son Alec, but she had a soft spot for her granddaughter's boyfriend. "Now I wouldn't mind seeing that man in coveralls and a wrench in his hand. Or even without coveralls and a wrench in his hand. Though I'm sure he would do just fine without the wrench."

Both women were silent as they contemplated the image of Chase Kingsley, dressed only in a wrench. Then Marge shook herself. It wasn't right to think of her potential future son-in-law that way. "Is he any good at plumbing, that's what I want to know."

"No idea, honey. But he can always come and clean my pipes, if you know what I mean."

Double ugh.

"Gotta go," said Mom. "Some old coot is yanking my chain. No, the doctor won't see you now, Cooper! You'll have to wait your turn!" she cried, then promptly disconnected.

Next on Marge's list of people to call in a case of an emergency was her daughter Odelia. Before she hired an expensive plumber and spent good money, she needed to exhaust all other—cheaper—possibilities, like any responsible homeowner would.

"Hey, Mom," said Odelia. "What's up?"

"Does Chase know anything about plumbing?"

"Does Chase know anything about plumbing? Well, he is pretty handy."

"Yes, but can he *fix* the plumbing?"

"Honestly? That exact theme never cropped up in any of our conversations."

"But what do you think?"

"I think you better ask Gwayn Partington. He's a licensed plumber."

A deep sigh. "Fine."

What good was it to have three men in the family when none of them could fix the plumbing? Maybe Odelia should have dated a handyman, not a cop. But her daughter was right. Why postpone the inevitable? So she dialed Gwayn

3

Partington's number and was gratified when the man picked up on the first ring.

"Hi, Gwayn. Marge Poole. When do you have time to take a look at my plumbing?"

"I could come over right now, if you want. I had another job lined up but that fell through, so…"

At that moment, her phone warned her that Odelia was trying to reach her, so she said, "One moment please, Gwayn. It's my daughter. Yes, honey?"

"I just called Chase and he says he doesn't know the first thing about plumbing and you better ask an expert if you ever want to enjoy the blessings of running water ever again."

"Thanks, honey," she said, and switched back to Gwayn. "Harrington Street 46. Yes, I'm home."

Ten minutes later Gwayn's van pulled to a stop in front of the house and when she opened the door she felt she'd done the right thing. Gwayn Partington did look amazingly capable, with his blue coveralls and his metal toolkit. At fifty he was pudgy and balding and maybe not the image of male perfection Chase Kingsley was, but at least he would get her faucets all working again, even though he might charge a small fortune.

And as he got down to business in the kitchen, she watched with an admiring eye how he didn't waste time. He fiddled with the tap, then disappeared underneath the sink for a moment, messed around there for a bit, and finally muttered something incomprehensible, took his toolkit and stomped down the stairs and into the basement.

Moments later he was stomping up again, went to grab something from his van and when he returned, soon the sounds of a hammer hitting a brick wall could be heard. Like a regular Thor fighting the demon that had messed up her plumbing, Gwayn swung a mean hammer.

No. This was not a problem Tex could have solved, or Alec, or even Chase.

And as she picked up a copy of *Women's World*, a holler at the front door made her put it down again. "You've got mail, lady!" the new arrival shouted.

She smiled as she got up to meet the mailwoman in the hallway.

"Hey, Bambi," she said as she joined her.

Bambi Wiggins had been their mailwoman for years, and was never too busy for a quick chat. And as she talked to Bambi about the new baby, and Bambi's husband Randi, suddenly a scream rose from the basement. Marge exchanged a look of concern with Bambi, and then both women were hurrying down the stairs. And as they came upon the licensed plumber, who was holding his hammer and chisel and staring at a hole he'd apparently made in the far wall, she asked, "What's wrong, Gwayn?"

The man looked a little greenish, and stood gnawing nervously at the end of his chisel. Already she knew what was going on here. He'd been a little hasty and had made a hole in the wrong place, possibly knocking out a load-bearing wall or a vital part of the house's plumbing system with one ill-advised blow of his hammer. And now, unlike Thor, he was too stunned and embarrassed to admit it.

And as she went in for a closer look, she suddenly halted in her tracks when her gaze fell upon a sight that couldn't possibly be real.

There, sitting and staring at her with its big sockets for eyes, was… a skeleton.

"Oh, my God," Bambi cried. "Marge. You've got a frickin' dead body in your wall!"

And so she had.

5

CHAPTER 1

*W*e were holding a war meeting in our war room. Well, maybe not a room, per se, but at least a war bush. Dooley, myself, Harriet and Brutus, the four cats that are part of the Poole family feline household, sat ensconced behind the tulip tree at the back of Odelia's backyard for this most important meeting. As befitting a war meeting of the war cabinet in the war bush, there was only one item on the agenda. A very important item.

Mice.

Yes, you read that right. I had called this most urgent and all-important meeting to discuss rodents. You may have seen them scurrying around in your basement or your attic, or even, for the more daring ones, in your kitchen, where they try to steal a piece of cheese, or, let's not limit ourselves to the clichés, a piece of beef or a slice of apple pie. After all, mice will eat almost anything their little hearts desire. As long as it's not too heavy they will carry it between their tiny rodent teeth and make off with it before you realize it's missing.

"We have to do it," said Brutus now, though he didn't seem entirely happy, just like the rest of us.

"I don't know, Brutus," said Harriet. "I don't like the idea of murder. And let's face it, that's what this is: pure and inexcusable homicide."

"Not homicide, though," I said. "Homicide means the murder of a person. A mouse is not a person. It's a rodent, so technically we're talking about rodenticide."

"I don't care what you call it, Max," said Harriet. "It's still a crime against humanity."

"Again, not a crime against humanity. Rodentity, possibly, if that's a word."

"I don't like this, Max," said Dooley, using a favorite phrase. "I don't want to kill mice. Mice are living creatures, just like the rest of us, and we should let them live in peace."

"Look, I'm all for letting mice live in peace and harmony," I said, "but the fact of the matter is that Odelia has given us an assignment, and we owe it to her to carry it out."

"First off, it wasn't Odelia that gave us the assignment," said Harriet. "It was Tex. And secondly, what can he do if we simply refuse to carry out his orders? Punish us? Hide our food? I don't think he'll do that, you guys. Tex is a doctor, not a monster."

"It wasn't just Tex," I said. "It was Marge, too. And I didn't hear Odelia or Gran or Chase complain when they told us to 'take care of the mouse problem,' did you?"

"If they want the mouse problem taken care of, they should do it themselves," said Harriet stubbornly. "We're cats, not hired assassins."

"It's common knowledge that cats catch mice," I explained.

"No, it's not."

"Yes, it is."

"It isn't!"

"I'm not a killer, Max," said Dooley. "And I don't want anything bad to happen to that sweet little mouse."

"I don't want anything bad to happen to the mouse either!" I said. "But it needs to go."

"So what if some nice Mickey Mouse chose Odelia's basement as its new home?" said Harriet. "Odelia should be happy. She should be glad. She should roll out the welcome mat! A new little friend for us to play with, and a source of joy for the Poole family."

"The mouse has been stealing food," I pointed out.

"Because it's hungry!"

"Maybe Odelia could feed it?" Dooley suggested it. "I wouldn't mind sharing some of my kibble with a sweet little Mickey Mouse."

"It's not a sweet little Mickey Mouse!" I said. "It's a thief, and if there's one there's probably others."

"I don't see the problem," said Harriet, shaking her head. "I really don't."

"Maybe we should go and talk to the mouse," Brutus now suggested.

"Exactly!" cried Harriet. "If Odelia really wants that mouse to behave, we should talk to the mouse and make it see reason. Tell it to say no to stealing. Reform. But then we also have to talk to Odelia and make her see reason, too. Tell her to adopt the mouse."

I rarely put my paws to my head but I did so now. "Adopt the mouse!" I cried.

"Why not? The Pooles love cats, why can't they learn to love mice, too?"

I leaned in. "Because they specifically told us to get rid of them!"

"We could always ask that sweet little mouse to move," Dooley now suggested. "That way we don't commit mousicide, and the Pooles will still be happy."

It seemed like an acceptable compromise, though I could tell Harriet wasn't entirely happy. "I'm still going to have a crack at Odelia and make her see the error of her mouse-hating ways," she said now.

"I think you're wrong," I said, drawing a hissed hush from Brutus. Never tell Harriet she's wrong, he clearly meant to say. But I was getting a little worked up myself.

Harriet drew her nose closer to mine, her eyes like slits. "And when have I ever been wrong about something?" she asked now.

She was going full Terminator on me now, and I almost expected her to shed her white furry skin and reveal the metal exoskeleton underneath.

"Okay, fine," I said, relenting. "But let's first have a chat with the mouse. And then you can have a crack at Odelia and the others."

"Great," said Harriet, smiling now that she'd gotten her way. "Let me talk to the mouse first, though. I'm sure I can convince it to play ball."

"What ball, Harriet?" asked Dooley, interested.

"Any ball!"

"You would expect that with four cats on the premises this mouse would have chosen another house to make its home," said Brutus.

"Maybe mice are not that smart?" Dooley suggested.

"Oh, I think mice are very smart," said Harriet. "Just look at Jerry. Jerry tricks Tom every time."

We all fell silent. In feline circles mentioning *Tom and Jerry* is considered sacrilege. A cat consistently being bested by a silly little mouse? That show has given cats a bad name. It has made people see us as lazy, dumb, vindictive, vicious and downright nasty. No, Messrs. Hanna and Barbera have a lot to answer for, let me tell you that.

We all moved back into the house, single file, then passed

through the pet flap. As usual I was the last one to pass through. There's a silent understanding among the Poole household cats that I always walk through the pet flap last. I'm big-boned, you see, and sometimes the flap refuses to cooperate with my particular bone structure. And as this impedes the free passage of my fellow cats, I'm always last. It was so now, and wouldn't you know it? I got stuck just as I tried to squeeze my midsection through that darn flap.

"Um, you guys?" I now called out. "Can you give a cat a helping paw here, please?"

"Oh, Max, not again!" cried Harriet, sounding exasperated.

"It's not my fault Odelia keeps feeding us primo grub!" I said.

We'd recently been catnapped, Dooley, Harriet, Brutus and I. In fact the entire cat population of Hampton Cove had been catnapped, and after that, to add insult to injury, we'd all been forced to eat vegetarian for a while, on account of the fact that the local populace had discovered they'd been fed cat and even human meat for a long time, an important ingredient in the local delicacy, the Duffer. The Duffer is—or was—a popular sausage, and its creators had taken a few liberties with food safety laws. As a consequence all of Hampton Cove had gone on a veggie kick, which hadn't lasted long.

Also, Vena, who is our veterinarian, and who seems to hate cats so much she likes to poke us with needles and pump us full of something called a vaccine, warned Odelia that cats shouldn't be deprived their daily ration of meat, or else they'll get sick and die.

Odelia had quickly seen the error of her ways and had started feeding us those wholesome nuggets of cat food again, kibble and pouches, and as a consequence I may have overindulged.

Or it could be a malfunction of the pet flap, of course. My money was on the latter.

Dooley took one of my paws, while Brutus took a firm grip on the other, and Harriet assumed the stance of the drill instructor that deep in her heart of hearts she is.

"And... pull!" she screamed. "And pull! And pull. Harder! Put your backs into it!"

"He's not moving!" Brutus cried.

"That's because you're not pulling hard enough, soldier!" she bellowed. "Pull! Pull!"

"I'm pulling as hard as I can!" said Dooley.

"Max, suck in that tummy. Suck it in!" Harriet yelled. "Suck! It! In!"

"Yeah, suck in that flab, Max!" said Brutus, panting from the exertion.

"I'll have you know I don't have any flab," I said haughtily, though it's hard to be haughty when you're stuck in a pet flap and two cats are pulling at your front paws with all of their might. "I'm as lean as that bowl of lean, mean turkey I just gobbled up."

"Less talk, more action!" Harriet was saying. "And pull and pull and pull!"

"I think the problem is that this here darn pet flap has shrunk," I said.

My two benefactors decided to take a short break and let go of my paws.

"Nonsense. You're fat, Max," said Harriet, never one to mince words. "You should go on a diet again."

"Pretty sure it's the flap," I said. "This door is made of wood, and everyone knows wood contracts when it gets cold and wet. It must have contracted. Like, a lot."

"How would this door get wet?" asked Brutus, puzzled.

"It gets really humid at night, Brutus," I pointed out. "Cold and humid."

"The sun has been up for hours. It's warm outside, Max," said Harriet. "So that theory doesn't hold water, I'm afraid. If anything that door should have expanded."

"Someone should go to the other side and push," said Dooley, not taking his eye off the ball, which in this case was me. "One of us could push while the other pulls."

"And how can we go to the other side when Max is blocking the exit?" asked Brutus.

"Maybe we can push from this side," said Harriet. "Make him pop out like a cork."

So the three of them put their paws on my face and started pushing!

"This isn't working," Brutus said after a while. "He's not moving an inch."

It wasn't a pleasant experience, three cats putting their paws on me and poking me in the snoot with all of their might. And Brutus was right. I wasn't budging. On the contrary. I had a feeling I was more stuck now than I was at the start of the proceedings.

And as we all contemplated our next move, I suddenly noticed we had a visitor. A very large mouse had casually strolled up to us and now sat watching the events as they unfolded before its pink whiskered nose.

"So this is what you cats are up to when you're not sleeping or eating or pooping, huh?" said the mouse with a slight grin on its face.

"We do a lot more than sleeping, eating and pooping," said Harriet.

"Oh, sure," said the mouse. "You're also supposed to be chasing me, but I see very little of that going on."

"We're not chasing you because we choose not to chase you," said Harriet. "Because we're all felinists at heart and respect the sanctity of rodent life."

"Yeah, we're vicious mouse hunters," said Brutus,

unsheathing a gleaming claw. "The only reason we haven't hunted you down is because we're not into that kind of stuff."

The mouse was studying its own teensy tiny claws, though, clearly not impressed. "You probably don't even know what those claws are for, you big brute."

"I know what these are for," said Brutus, and now showed his fangs, then even managed to make a hissing sound that sounded very menacing and convincing to me.

The mouse produced a slight smile. "You huff and you puff but you can't even get through that silly little pet door, so forgive me for not being too impressed, fellas."

And with that parting shot, the mouse started back in the direction of the basement stairs, which apparently was its new home. At least according to the Pooles.

"We should probably…" Brutus began, giving Harriet a hesitant look.

"Talk to it!" said Harriet. "We agreed to talk to the mouse so let's talk to the mouse."

Brutus cleared his throat. "Um, mouse? Come back here, will you?"

"That's Mr. Mouse to you, cat," said the mouse, glancing over his shoulder.

"Um, the thing is…" Brutus darted another glance at Harriet, who gave him an encouraging nod. "We've actually been asked to tell you that you're no longer welcome in this house. So if you could please move to some other house that would be really nice."

"Well done," Harriet said with an approving smile. "Very felinistic."

But the mouse laughed. "You're telling me to take a hike? You've got some nerve, cat."

"We happen to live here," said Brutus, stiffening visibly.

"And as the co-inhabitants of this house we have every right to ask you to clear out and to clear out right speedily, too."

"Well said, sugar muffin," said Harriet, who seemed to be hardening her stance. Whereas before she'd been a strong defender of rodent rights, she was now eyeing the mouse with a lot more frost than a rodent rights activist should.

"Well, for your information, I like this place, so I'm staying put. And there's nothing you or your dumb chum cat cronies can do about it. So buzz off already, will you?"

"Oh, we'll see about that," said Brutus, finally losing his equanimity. And then he performed the feline equivalent of rolling up his sleeves: he rolled his shoulders and extended his claws. I would have helped him square off against this obnoxious little mouse, but unfortunately I was still stuck in the pet flap, and being stuck has a strangely debilitating effect on one's fighting spirit. Still, he had my most vocal support.

"You don't scare me, cat," said the mouse. "If you want a fight, I'll give you a fight."

"Don't be stupid, mouse," said Harriet, the master diplomat. "We're ten times bigger than you. We can squash you like a bug, and we will if you don't get out of our house."

The mouse wasn't impressed. "It's true that you're bigger than me, cat. But you're also a lot dumber. Besides, much of that size is flab, like your fat red friend who's stuck in that pet flap can tell you, and why should I be scared of a bunch of hairy butterballs? Now if there's nothing more, I've got things to do, mice to see, so cheerio, suckers."

And with these fighting words, he was off, scurrying back to wherever he came from.

He left four cats fuming. Or actually one cat fuming (Brutus), one cat wondering how to get out of the pet flap (yours truly), one cat counting on his digits how much bigger than a mouse a cat could possibly be (Dooley) and one cat looking like the Terminator about to go full metal menace (Harriet).

"Oh, I'll show that little jerk what's what," Harriet hissed. Apparently rodent rights were suddenly the furthest thing from her mind. And as she stalked off in the direction of the basement stairs, Brutus right behind her, I wondered how I was ever going to get out of my pet flap predicament now.

"I think we're actually thirty times bigger than a mouse, Max, or maybe even more. What do you think?"

"I think I want to get out of here," I said.

"I think the situation will take care of itself."

"You mean the mouse situation?"

"No, your situation. If you simply stay stuck for a while and don't eat, you'll automatically get thinner and get unstuck before you know it."

And having delivered this message of hope, he plunked down on his haunches, and gave me a smile, entirely ready to keep me company while I accomplished this rare feat.

"It will take me days to slim down and get unstuck, though," I said, pointing out the fatal flaw in his reasoning.

"I don't think so. A lot of weight gain is fluids," said Dooley. "So the key is to get dehydrated." He nodded wisely. "You need to sweat, Max, and sweat a lot. And then all of that extra weight will simply melt away."

And to show me he wasn't all talk and no action, he got up, jumped on top of the kitchen table, flicked the thermostat to Maximum, and jumped back down again.

"There," he said, satisfied with a job well done. "It's going to turn into a sauna in here and you'll be free before you know it." He gave me a reassuring pat on the head.

Odd, then, that I wasn't entirely reassured.

CHAPTER 2

*O*ver at the office, Tex was watering his spider plant while listening to the radio. He'd turned up the volume, as the song that was playing happened to be one of his favorites. It was a golden oldie from that old master of melody Elton John. And as he sang the lyrics, exercising the old larynx, he suddenly realized how much he actually liked to sing.

"Humpty Dumpty doo wah doo wah," he warbled softly.

The spider plant was one of his favorites. He'd gotten it as a present from his daughter a couple of years ago, after she'd been in to see him about a suspicious mole that had developed on the back of her hand, and had told him his office looked dark and gloomy and could use sprucing up. In the week that followed she'd assumed the role of head of the sprucing-up committee and had redesigned his office, making it lighter and airier.

It had been her idea to put in the skylight, and to throw out the old rug that had developed a strange odor after years of use. She'd had the original wood floor sanded and refinished so it shone when the sun cast its golden rays through the new skylight, and as a finishing touch had thrown out his old furniture and replaced it with a nice and modern-looking desk and chair. Now the office didn't look like it belonged to a nineteenth-century sawbones but a modern young physician hip with the times.

"Doo wah doo wah," he sang, louder now that he decided that he had a pretty great singing voice. "Doo wah doo wee wee weeh…"

O n the other side of the door, Vesta was watching a YouTube video on her phone. There were no patients in the waiting room, and no patients in with Tex either, so she had all the time in the world. But this video was something else. And as she watched, suddenly a horrible noise intruded on her viewing pleasure. It sounded like a cross between the howl of a wolf and the yowl of a cat in heat. It took her a while to trace the source of the sound, and when she had, she got up and marched over to the door.

Without knocking, she opened it and stuck her head in.

"Tex? Are you all right?" she asked, showing a solicitude she rarely displayed when dealing with her son-in-law.

"I'm fine," said Tex, looking up from watering his plant. "Why?"

She shook her head. "The weirdest thing. I thought I heard someone being mangled by a timber wolf but now it stopped."

"You're imagining things, Vesta, cause I heard nothing."

"Yeah, that must be it," she murmured, then made to close the door, only to push it open again. "Say, have you ever considered we may be about to be annihilated, Tex?"

"Mh?" he said, looking up from plucking something from his precious plant.

"The coming apocalypse," she explained. "I was just watching a great video about the coming apocalypse and what we should do to get ready for when it comes."

"What apocalypse?" he asked, getting up and staring at whatever he'd plucked from his plant.

"The one that's about to start. There's a nuclear holocaust about to happen, Tex, or hadn't you noticed?"

"No, actually I hadn't. What nuclear holocaust?"

"Well, it only stands to reason that with so many nuclear weapons in the world someone is gonna launch one any second now, and that someone may be a rogue agent, or it may be a rogue nation, or it may be a rogue organization. Something rogue at any rate. And then there's the tsunamis that are about to rock our world, not to mention the volcanoes that are about to go active, and the rising oceans. We need to get ready, Tex. It's imperative we build ourselves a bunker and store it with enough food to survive this thing."

He gave her a strange look. "Vesta, there's not going to be a nuclear holocaust. The people in charge will never let that happen. And as far as those oceans and those volcanoes are concerned, I'm sure it will all be fine."

"All be fine! You sound like those animals that stick their heads in the sand! Kangaroos? No, ostriches." She pointed a finger at him. "You, Tex, are an ostrich, and it's because of ostriches that things are quickly going to hell in a handbasket."

"Uh-huh," he said, not sounding all that interested. "What do you think these are?" he asked, staring at his own finger like the ding-dong he was. "Is that a bug, you think, or a fungus?"

"Oh, you're a fungus, Tex," she said, and slammed the door shut.

It didn't matter. Even though Tex was a lost cause, that didn't mean she couldn't take matters into her own hands.

Wasn't that always the case, though? Didn't it always come down to simple, honest, hard-working women to get the job done?

So she got behind her desk, took pen and paper in hand, and started scribbling down a list of things she needed to get cracking on to survive this coming nuclear winter.

ﻬ

"*I*t's been in there an awfully long time," said Uncle Alec, staring at the skeleton.

"And how long is an awfully long time?" asked Odelia. "In your expert opinion?"

"Heck, honey, I'm just a cop, not a coroner. So I have absolutely no idea."

"I'll bet it's been in there a thousand years," said Marge. "Look at the state it's in."

"I doubt it's been a thousand years, though, Marge," said Chase. "This house isn't a thousand years old."

"So what? It could have been there from way before this house was ever built."

"Impossible, mom," said Odelia. "It's in the wall, so it was put there after the house was built."

"Oh," said Marge. "You think?"

"I'm not an expert either, but yeah, that's what I think."

"Abe should be here any minute now," said Alec, checking his watch. "We'll know more when he arrives."

Abe Cornwall was the county coroner, and as such more qualified than any of the small band of onlookers who now stood gathered around the skeleton, staring at it as if hoping it would magically reveal its secrets somehow.

"I still don't have water," Marge pointed out. Her initial shock had worn off.

Odelia placed a hand on her mother's shoulder. "Don't worry, mom. As soon as the body is taken out, I'm sure the plumber will be able to get the water running again."

"Yeah, but the laundry still needs to be done, and I need to cook, and I wanted to mop the floors—though now with all these people running in and out of the basement I guess it's not much use anyway."

"If you want you and Dad and Gran can eat at ours tonight."

"Thanks," said Marge. "But what about showers tomorrow morning?"

"You can take a shower at ours, as well."

"Thanks, sweetie," said Marge, biting her lip nervously.

"So Gwayn took a whack at this wall and this skeleton popped up," said Alec, jotting down a couple of notes.

"Yeah, Gwayn figured there was an issue with the connection to the water main—a leak maybe—so he wanted to take a closer look before he called in the people from the water company. And that's when this old skeleton suddenly popped up," said Marge.

Gwayn Partington had gone home already. Or, as was more likely, to his favorite bar.

"Clothes are mostly gone, too," said Alec. "Though they look like a man's clothes to me."

The skeleton had a few rags draped around itself. It was hard to see what they'd been, though, in spite of what Odelia's uncle said. Everything looked old and ragged.

"Look, just get it out of here, will you?" said Marge. "So I can call Gwayn and he can fix my plumbing and I have water again." And with these words she moved up the stairs.

"So how long do you really think it's been there, Uncle Alec?" asked Odelia.

"Hard to say, sweetie. These houses were built in the

fifties, so it has to be less than that, and bodies take a little while to turn into skeletons, so it can't be recent, either. But like I said, it's up to the experts to tell us the age of the body, or how it died."

"And how it got stuck inside this wall," Chase added.

"But it didn't get stuck inside the wall, did it?" said Odelia. "Someone put it there."

Alec moved a little closer and stuck his head in to look up. "Yeah, doesn't look like a chimney or anything, so it's definitely not some wannabe Santa who got stuck."

"Ha ha," said Odelia. "Very funny."

"No, it happens," said Alec, retracting his head. "I once heard about a case where a guy went missing. Years later a house in the same neighborhood was sold and when the builders came in to do some remodeling they found a body stuck inside the old chimney. Turns out he'd been burgling the house and had gotten stuck and died."

"You know what this means, right?" said Odelia.

"What?"

"This is a murder case."

"A murder case!" said Alec.

"Of course. What else could it be?"

"Anything! A very elaborate suicide. An accident. Um…"

"It's murder, and whoever put this poor person in there managed to get away with it for all this time."

"Oh, don't tell me you think we should…" Alec began.

"Investigate who killed him or her? Of course. It doesn't matter if it happened yesterday or fifty years ago, we need to get to the bottom of this."

"But—"

"There's people out there who lost a brother, a sister or a mother or a father. And who never had closure. People who want to know what happened, and who deserve answers, and to see justice done. And the murderer is probably still out there, happy they got away with it. Well, I would like you to promise me you're not going to let that happen. That you're going to do whatever it takes to bring this person to justice."

CHAPTER 3

"*I*'m getting very hot, Dooley," I said.

As you may or may not know, cats don't sweat, unless it's through the soles of their paws. But since the available acreage for sweating is so limited we usually seek other ways of cooling our overheated bodies down, like placing ourselves on top of a cold surface, seeking shade, or drinking cooling liquids. But since none of those avenues were available to me, I was suffering.

"That means it's working, Max," said Dooley. "Just hang in there."

I was frankly melting, so if that's what Dooley meant when he said it was working he was probably right. But I was still stuck in that door, and if anything I had the feeling I was expanding, not shrinking.

"I think you've got this all wrong, Dooley," I said. "I shouldn't be heating up, I should be cooling down. Physical objects exposed to heat expand, and when exposed to cold, they contract. So you should be turning down the heat and turning up the AC full blast."

He thought about this. "There's something in that," he

admitted. "So what are you saying, Max? That we should turn this house into a freezer?"

"I think what I'm saying is that I'm about to expire," I said, puffing some more. "And if you don't turn off the heat you won't even have to bother getting me out of this door. The county coroner will do it for you before arresting you for murder by central heating."

"Just hang in there a little bit longer," he encouraged me. "I'm sure it's working. Have you tried to move again?"

"Yes, Dooley. What do you think I've been doing? I'm completely stuck!"

"Let me give it another try," he said, and put his paws on my nose and pushed.

"Owowowow!" I said.

"What?" he asked, pausing to listen to my complaint.

"Retract your claws already, will you?!"

"Oops, sorry. Force of habit." So he tried again, only this time without claws.

"It's not working!" I cried as I wriggled to get some traction.

"Uncle Alec should have made that door a lot bigger," said Dooley, giving up.

"Uncle Alec, Tex and Chase," I said.

For a moment, we both lay there, staring at each other, then he said, "I've got it. Repeat after me, Max. 'Every day, in every way, I'm getting thinner and thinner and thinner.'"

"Every day, in every way, I'm getting thinner and thinner and thinner," I said.

"Now say it like you believe it!" he said, like a regular new age guru. "And try to visualize yourself getter thinner, too. The power of the mind, Max. It's all about the power of the mind. I saw it on the Discovery Channel. This is what Olympic athletes do. Before they start their routine they visualize success. Picture it in their minds."

"Every day, in every way..." I muttered. Just then, the door started moving. My eyes popped open. "It's working!" I cried. "I'm not doing anything and my body is moving!"

Unfortunately it wasn't me popping out of that door as if nudged by the invisible hand of Louise Hay, but someone actually opening the door. And since the door swung inwards, any moment now I could be squashed between door and kitchen wall.

Lucky for me Dooley had the presence of mind to yell, "Stop! You're squishing Max!"

My progress towards the wall halted, and I heaved a sigh of extreme relief.

"Max!" said Odelia, for it was she. "What are you doing down there?"

"I'm making a study of the floor," I said. "What do you think I'm doing? Your uncle, dad and boyfriend made this door much too small."

"He got stuck again," said Dooley.

"I knew it," said Odelia, crouching down and placing her hands underneath my armpits. "I should never have fed you all of that soft food. I knew it would make you balloon up in size again."

"I'm not a balloon!" I cried. "The door has shrunk since the last time I passed through."

With expert hands she pulled, and finally the flap released its hold on me.

"You did it!" cried Dooley. "You saved him!"

"I don't know about that," said Odelia, "but at least he's not stuck in the door anymore. How long have you been down there?"

"Oh, just a couple of minutes," I said.

"Over an hour," said Dooley.

"And why is it so hot in here?"

"That was my idea," said Dooley. "I turned up to heat so Max would lose weight."

"Dehydration, huh? Clever pussy," said Odelia as she gave Dooley a pat on the head.

He looked like a million bucks while I merely gave him a dirty look. I was the one who'd practically sweat his entire body weight out through his paws and was now leaving soggy paw prints all across the kitchen floor. I made a beeline for my water bowl and began to drink with big, greedy gulps.

"We found a dead body, you guys," said Odelia.

"A dead body?" I asked. "Where? Who? Why?"

"Well, a dead skeleton, to be more precise. And I want you to sniff around and try to figure out whose skeleton it might be, and how long it's been stuck there." She was rooting through a kitchen drawer in search of something. "So ask around, will you? I know the house next door used to belong to the Bakers, but I doubt they were the first owners. Besides, I don't think the Bakers were capable of murder, or burying a body in their basement. My family have known the Bakers for a long time and they're not killers."

"Is this a new case, Odelia?" asked Dooley.

"Yes, a cold case," she said.

I was in desperate need of a cold spot to sit, but I refrained from mentioning this.

"A cold case?" asked Dooley. "Because the body is cold, you mean?"

"No, because the case has probably been dropped by the police a long time ago, if it was ever a case at all. It could be that no one ever bothered to report this person missing, in which case we don't even know who they might be."

"Sounds very complicated," I grumbled. I was in no mood to take on a case, cold or otherwise, having just suffered through such a harrowing and embarrassing ordeal.

"Well, you're going to have to help me," she said. "Ah, I've found it." She picked what looked like an old diary from the kitchen drawer.

"What's that, Odelia?" asked Dooley.

"My old diary. I remember once wanting to write a story about the history of this neighborhood, and doing some preliminary research, before Dan told me to drop the story." She opened the old diary and sat down at the kitchen table. "Can you turn down that thermostat, Dooley? It's like an oven in here."

Dooley did as he was told, and Odelia frowned as she studied her notes.

"This entire block of houses was built in the early fifties," she said. "One of the first neighborhoods of its kind ever to be built in this part of Hampton Cove, in fact."

"Maybe Dan remembers who lived here in the fifties?" I suggested.

"Or Gran," said Dooley. "She's probably as old as the house. Or older."

Odelia smiled. "Don't let her hear you say that. Gran is very sensitive about her age. But you're right. Gran may know something we don't, and so may Dan." She got up. "I'm going next door again. I want to be there when the coroner shows up to take that skeleton out of the wall. Meanwhile, I want you guys to go out there and find out anything you can about that house and its occupants. Anything that might help us figure out what happened." And as she moved to the door, she added, "Oh, and Max? Please don't try to fit through the pet door again. I'll open the window. You can come and go that way."

"But isn't that dangerous?" said Dooley, wide-eyed. "A burglar could get in."

She laughed. "Oh, Dooley. I think I can take that chance. After all, there hasn't been a burglary in this neighborhood in years. Besides, I'll come and close the window before I leave for work."

And with these words she let me and Dooley out, and then closed the door, but not before opening the glass sliding door to the living room a crack.

And then Dooley and I were on our way, a new investigation to sink our teeth into, and a reprieve from our old assignment, which Odelia seemed to have forgotten about.

"No more mice to get rid of, Max," said Dooley happily, having reached the same conclusion.

"And a good thing, too," I said.

We bumped paws, and then we were off, ready to tackle this newest assignment.

CHAPTER 4

"*I*'m not so sure about this, Jerry," said Johnny Carew, leaning across the steering wheel of the van and looking out at the house they were currently staking out.

"You don't have to be sure, you moron," said his friend and partner in crime Jerry Vale. "As long as I'm sure that's what matters."

"Uh-huh," said Johnny. He was a bear of a man, while Jerry looked more like a scrawny chicken. They'd been friends and colleagues for a very long time.

"Can you explain the plan to me again?" asked Johnny. "I think I missed something."

"You didn't miss something," growled Jerry, who was in a foul mood. "You probably missed everything. Look, if we're gonna do this, we need to know what the cops are like in this godforsaken town, all right?"

"Uh-huh," said Johnny, taking this information and storing it in his brain, such as it was.

"So we pull off a minor B&E and see how fast the local fuzz gets here, see?"

"Yup," said Johnny. "But what if they get here real fast, Jer? What if they get here so fast they catch us and throw our ass in jail? I don't wanna go back to jail, Jer. Nuh-uh."

"They won't throw our ass in jail. Not for a minor little thing like this. And even if we get caught, which is unlikely, because nobody cares about some shitty little house in a shitty little neighborhood like this with so many multi-million-dollar mansions to protect, we can always tell 'em we thought it was our own place and we made a mistake."

"You think they'll buy that?"

"If the local fuzz are as dumb as I think they are? Sure."

"I still wish Chazz hadn't kicked us out, Jer."

"Yeah, well, that can't be helped, Johnny. The big guy did what he thought was right, and I'm sure he's already sorry he acted so rash."

"You really think so, Jer? You think he's sorry he canned us?"

"Sure! We were the best he got! And even more than that, we shared a bond."

"We did. We really did."

Chazz Falcone, the man they used to work for, was one of the richest men in the country, known for his real estate deals and the empire he built in his home town of New York. Johnny and Jerry had worked for the guy for so long they considered Chazz family. At first they'd been hired muscle to put the squeeze on stubborn tenants who needed to get muscled out of the buildings Chazz bought for a bargain so he could tear them down and build one of his high-rise monoliths. They'd graduated to important positions on Chazz's staff when the latter had decided to run for president, and when that hadn't worked out, Johnny had become Chazz's dog handler, and Jerry the man's dietician.

Unfortunately Johnny and Jerry were old crooks who had a hard time keeping to the straight and narrow, so when the opportunity presented itself to dip their hands into the company till, they hadn't held back and had dipped with abandon and obvious glee.

Chazz hadn't been happy when he found out and had immediately terminated their employment. And since they'd been forced to pay back every penny they pinched, they now found themselves on a road they thought they'd left behind: graciously allowing other, more law-abiding citizens, to pay for their way of life. And because the Hamptons were a place they knew well, and where a lot of money was located on an area the size of a postage stamp, they now found themselves back on their old stomping ground.

They watched as a car drew up to the house next to the one they were targeting, and when a fat man stepped out carrying a small suitcase, Jerry said, "Looks like a doctor."

"Yeah, has to be a doctor," Johnny agreed.

"Weird, though, right? People have been coming and going in the place next door, but ours hasn't seen any sign of life yet. At least if you don't count the two cats that came hotfooting it out from behind it."

"I like cats," said Johnny. "I think cats are a good sign, Jer. A good omen."

Jerry muttered something about what he thought of omens and where Johnny could stick them. He hunkered down in his seat and watched the house with eyes half-closed.

"So when do we strike, Jer?" asked Johnny, rubbing his hands. Now that he'd decided this was a pretty solid plan, he couldn't wait to get started.

"Tonight," said Jerry as he closed his eyes. "Tonight's the night, Johnny. So keep your eyes peeled, will you?"

And as Johnny did as he was told, Jerry's chin dropped to his chest and soon he was snoring like a chainsaw.

From behind Johnny a little dog came snuffling, then

climbed onto Johnny's lap. It was Spot, one of the dogs Johnny had dog-watched for Chazz. As a parting gift, and proving that he had his heart in the right place, in spite of being betrayed by his two associates, Chazz had gifted Johnny the dog he loved so much.

"Hey, little buddy," said Johnny. "So do you like cats, too?"

Spot barked a curt bark of agreement.

"Oh, I thought you would. You love those funny-looking creatures, do you? Do you, buddy? Huh?"

Spot barked happily. He did, he did!

"Will you shut that dog up already," Jerry growled without opening his eyes.

"Shush, Spot," said Johnny, placing a sausage-sized index finger to Spot's lips. "Daddy is napping, so we must be very quiet now, you hear?"

Spot seemed to smile, but didn't bark, showing what a clever little doggie he was.

And then Johnny gave himself up to silent surveillance, something he was very good at. So good, in fact, that five minutes later he was fast asleep, his deep and regular snores competing with Jerry's for volume and pitch.

CHAPTER 5

"Come out of there, mouse," said Harriet. "And if you don't come out I will…" She hesitated. Brutus gave her a questioning look. What would she do if the mouse refused to leave its hiding place in the walls of Odelia's basement? She couldn't very well crawl in there and bodily drag it out. She was too big for that, and the mouse entirely too small.

"We'll smoke you out," said Brutus, having a bright idea.

She rolled her eyes. "How are we going to smoke it out?"

"Well, with smoke," he suggested.

"And how do we do that? Do you have something to create smoke?"

"No, but Odelia has, and she'll only be too happy to give us credit for the idea."

"Humans don't like it when you set their house on fire, Brutus," she said, with a little less than her usual warmth and affection, "on account of the fact that when their house burns down they don't have a place to stay. Which means we don't have a place to stay."

"But we get rid of the mouse," he said with a grin.

She gave him the kind of look that quickly made him lose the grin.

"If you don't come out right this instance," she said as inspiration finally struck, "I'm going to lock the door of the basement and you'll be trapped down here, without food or water until you agree to leave."

A laugh suddenly sounded from nearby. She immediately leaped to its source and saw that it had come from a tiny little hole in the wall right behind the big furnace.

"Who cranked up the heat like that?" said Brutus as he puffed a little. "That furnace has been blasting away non-stop since we came down those stairs."

He was right. For some reason the furnace was working overtime, emitting a dry heat that was searing Harriet's sensitive features.

"You don't get it, do you, cat?" said a voice from within the wall. "We don't need doors. We move around this house and never use any of those passageways humans like to use, or cats."

"He's right," said Brutus. "Mice are notoriously clever little creatures. They can probably move through the walls and reach any part of the house without being seen."

"So how do we fight the annoying critters?!"

"You can't!" said the mouse from within the safety of the wall. "Just accept it, cat. We're here to stay. Now beat it. I'm trying to take a nap and you're bothering me."

In response, Harriet moved fast as lightning and jammed her paw into the tiny hole. "Come here, you annoying little beast!" she cried. For a moment she thought she could feel something soft and squishy being impaled by her sharp claws. But when she retracted her paw she saw it was just a piece of old styrofoam.

"Beat it, you stupid cat!" said the mouse. "You'll never catch me. Never, you hear? Never, never, never!"

And with these words, suddenly a piece of cheese was projected from the tiny hole. It wasn't so much a piece of cheese as a rind, though, neatly nibbled down to the plastic. It hit Harriet right on the nose.

"Oh, you horrible little…" she growled.

"Oh, well," said Brutus, who didn't seem overly concerned by the cheek of the cheese-eating little mite. "Live and let live, right? So maybe we should go back upstairs? I'm burning up down here. Place is turning into a sauna."

"I'll get you!" Harriet cried, shaking her paw. "If it's the last thing I do, I'll get you, you stupid mouse!"

The sound of laughter echoed through the basement, and this time, even though she tried to locate its source so she could jam her paw in and grab the miscreant, it could have come from anywhere. The mouse was right: it moved through the walls like a ghost.

"Let's go," said Brutus again, "before we both melt."

Grudgingly, Harriet agreed. And they were moving up the wooden staircase to the door when it suddenly slammed shut. And when they tried to shove it open, they couldn't!

"Great," said Harriet. "And now we can't get out."

"Take that, cat!" the mouse shouted, and tiny little feet could be heard scurrying away from the basement door.

"Did he do that?" asked Harriet. "Did he really lock us up down here?"

"Looks like," said Brutus. A tiny smile lifted the corners of his mouth. "Clever little…" He swallowed the rest of the sentence when Harriet threw him a furious look. "Nasty critter," he muttered instead, and hunkered down at the foot of the stairs.

They'd have to wait it out, until Odelia found them missing, and decided to go look for them. Until then, they were prisoners down there.

Prisoners of a mouse. How absolutely embarrassing was that?

&.

*O*delia was glad to finally see Abe Cornwall arrive. The big guy with the mass of frizzy hair was panting as he lumbered down the stairs into the basement. "So what do we have here?" he asked, ducking for a low-hanging wooden beam and then again for the canoe Tex had once stored there and promptly forgotten about.

"A body," said Uncle Alec dryly. "But a very peculiar one."

"Oh, goodie," said Abe, rubbing his hands as he caught sight of the skeleton.

This was what Howard Carter must have felt like when he entered Tutankhamen's tomb, Odelia thought. The coroner actually looked thrilled with this new assignment.

He moved closer and eyed the body from top to toe. "Oh, yes," he said. "Yes, yes, yes."

"Well?" said Alec finally, when the doctor had muttered as much as he seemed willing to. "What can you tell us about the poor bastard?"

"Not much, I'm afraid," said Abe. "In fact there isn't anything I can tell you right now, apart from the fact that it's a human being and not a dog or a cat."

"Yeah, well, I could have told you that," said Alec. "But how long has it been here? And how did he or she die—and is it a she or a he?"

"I'd say it's a male, judging from the width of the pelvis, the shape of the jawbone and the length of the long bones, but to be absolutely certain I'll have to take this fine specimen back to my lab and perform a series of tests on it." He was actually rubbing his hands now, in obvious glee. "I'll call in my team. They'll be absolutely thrilled."

"So when will you be able to tell us something?"

"Not soon, Alec," said Abe. "Though of course I'll do my best for you." He suddenly frowned and moved in for a closer look, using a small penlight. "Will you look at that," he murmured, and then they all moved in closer. The coroner's light shone down into the space between the two walls, and hit something shiny and glittering located at the feet of the body. And as the coroner carefully lifted it from its hiding place, Odelia gasped when she saw what it was: a diamond brooch. Very large, and obviously very, very valuable… "Ta-dah," Abe said with satisfaction, like a magician pulling a rabbit from a hat.

CHAPTER 6

"So how are we supposed to find out who that body belonged to?" asked Dooley.

"Good question, Dooley," I said. "And I have absolutely no answer for you."

We were walking along the sidewalk, pretty much going where the wind led us. Odelia and Marge and Tex's houses are part of a neighborhood of similar houses. Maybe not tract housing, necessarily, but since they were all built around the same time they all look similar in design and construction. Both Marge and Odelia's houses, for instance, have a small entrance, that leads straight into the living room, a sitting room now mainly used to watch television and in the olden days where people entertained their guests.

The living room is also the dining room, though not in Odelia's house, since she usually eats in the kitchen, which is connected to the living room. Off the kitchen is the laundry room. Upstairs there are three more rooms and a bathroom: the master bedroom where Odelia and Chase sleep, and of course me and Dooley, though sometimes Dooley favors Grandma's bed in the house next door. Then there's the guest bedroom, which Odelia and Chase are converting to an office slash home gym, and then finally there's a small room where Odelia stores a lot of her junk. It's filled with all the stuff she can't fit in the rest of the house. Oh, and there's also a crawl space she calls an attic, and a basement, which apparently has become the home of a mouse or mice.

We wandered idly through the neighborhood, trying to come up with a plan of campaign.

"No animal is old enough to have witnessed the events that killed that person," I said.

"We don't even know how old it is," Dooley pointed out.

"He must be younger than the house, though, or else how would he have managed to get stuck in its basement?"

"How do you know it's a he?"

"Just a hunch. Only men are dumb enough to get stuck inside a basement wall."

"True," Dooley admitted. "Harriet would never allow herself to be trapped like that."

"I think I once read that the oldest living organism on the planet is a fungus," I said.

"So where do we find a fungus to interview?"

"Not sure. And I'm not even sure Mr. or Mrs. Fungus would want to talk to us. I hear they're very private organisms."

We both lapsed into silence. This was a tough assignment Odelia had given us. One of those impossible missions Tom Cruise likes so much. Only Tom's missions usually end up with him dangling from high-speed trains, skyscrapers or the outsides of airplanes. At least our mission didn't involve that kind of hair-raising stunt. At least I hoped it wouldn't. I'm not all that keen on hair-raising stunts, and I don't think Dooley is either.

We'd ambled along through the neighborhood without meeting a single fungus and decided to wend our way into town. There are always fellow cats to be found downtown, and maybe they'd be able to give us some ideas. Show us in the right direction.

We took a left turn at the end of the next street and saw a very old cat lying in the window of a house. It opened one eye to give us a curious glance, then closed it again. Apparently it didn't like what it saw, for it went on sleeping as if we weren't even there.

"How old do cats get, Max?" asked Dooley now.

It was a point I'd often wondered about myself. "I honestly don't know, Dooley," I said. "Though I'm guessing very old. We're very wise creatures, you know, and wise creatures usually get very, very old."

"I think so too," Dooley agreed. "I once saw this documentary about how the Egyptians loved cats so much they thought they came from the gods, and we all know that gods can get very old indeed."

"I know, just look at their beards. Only very old beings have beards like that."

We'd arrived on the outskirts of downtown Hampton Cove and decided to go in search of the feline mayor of our town, a title worn with pride by Kingman, a voluminous piebald who likes to hold forth on Main Street, in front of his owner's general store. When we arrived, Kingman was dozing on top of the checkout counter, while his human Wilbur Vickery was busy ringing up his customers' purchases.

I cleared my throat. "Hey, Kingman."

He opened his eyes and yawned. "Oh, hey, guys. How's it hanging?"

Dooley looked at me, I looked at him, and then we both looked at Kingman.

"How is what hanging?" I asked.

"How should I know? It's an expression."

"Oh, right," I said. I'm not always hip to the finer points of the feline language, even though I am a feline myself. I wasn't going to let that stop me from asking a most important question, though. "What is the oldest animal in Hampton Cove, Kingman?"

He thought about his for a moment, then said, "I guess that would be Camilla."

"Who is Camilla?" asked Dooley.

"Camilla is a bird, and not just any bird, mind you. Camilla is a macaw, and currently lives with her owner out on Morley Street. Why do you want to know?"

"Marge found a body in her basement," said Dooley.

"Well, not a body," I said. "A skeleton."

"A skeleton is a body, though, right, Max?"

"No, a body is more than just a skeleton, a body still has all of its fixtures attached."

"The juicy bits," Kingman confirmed. "A skeleton is a body without the juicy bits."

"Oh," said Dooley, nodding. "You mean like a fishbone after we eat the meat?"

"Yeah, exactly like a fishbone," I said.

"So a body, huh?" said Kingman. "Why is it that the Pooles keep stumbling over bodies everywhere they go?"

"Not a body," I said. "A skeleton."

"Same difference. It must have belonged to a human once, right? And that human is now presumably dead?"

"I would think so," I said. "I didn't see the skeleton but I imagine it wasn't jumping around and dancing the hornpipe."

"So who is it?" asked Kingman. "Anyone I know?"

"Odelia seems to think it must have been there for a very long time, possibly many decades," I said. "And now she wants us to figure out who it could have belonged to."

"Many decades, huh? Now I see why you want to find the

oldest animal in town. Well, your best bet will be Camilla, though there are other, maybe even older organisms, of course. Mollusks tend to get very old, too."

"Mollusks?"

"Sure. The oldest known clam lived to be over five hundred years."

"A clam, huh?"

"I doubt whether a clam would be able to tell us a lot about the skeleton in Marge's basement, though," said Dooley, echoing my thoughts exactly.

"Yeah, I guess you may have a point," Kingman conceded.

"Well, thanks, Kingman," I said. "And if you find out anything else about the former owners of Tex and Marge's house, you will let us know, right?"

"Sure thing, boys," said Kingman, and promptly dozed off again.

"Kingman must have had a rough night," said Dooley as we walked on. "He seemed more sleepy than usual."

"He was probably up all night chasing mice," I said. "Kingman loves to chase mice."

"Most cats love to chase mice," said Dooley. "We're the only ones that don't. Why is that, Max?"

"Um, I guess we're the only cats with a moral compass?"

"I wonder if Harriet and Brutus have caught the mouse in Odelia's basement."

"I'll bet she has. Harriet seemed dead set on catching that mouse."

"Poor Mr. Mouse," said Dooley, shaking his head in dismay.

"Are you actually rooting for the creature now, Dooley?"

"I am. We are all members of God's great flock, Max, and I feel for that poor thing, with Harriet on his tail, trying to eat him at every turn. I'll bet that poor Mr. Mouse is scared stiff right now, running for his life and wondering where the next attack will come from, and then, just before the final blow lands, looking into Mrs. Mouse's eyes, and together gazing at all of their sweet little baby mice..."

My heart sank at Dooley's words. Poor Mr. Mouse. Poor Mrs. Mouse. Poor baby mice.

"We have to save that mouse, Max," he said. "What are those precious little baby mice going to do when Harriet and Brutus have brutally slain and eaten their mom and dad?"

The picture Dooley had painted was so poignant I felt compelled to wipe away a tear. "I think it's probably too late, Dooley," I said. "That poor mouse has probably gotten it in the neck by now."

"That poor, poor Mr. Mouse," he said in sad lament.

CHAPTER 7

"*T*hat horrible, horrible mouse!" Harriet was yelling as she stomped around the basement, furious.

"Maybe we should preserve our energy," Brutus suggested. "We could be down here for a long time."

"I can't believe this. Imagine what the members of cat choir are going to say when they find out we've been bested by a stupid little mouse. They're going to turn us into the laughingstock of Hampton Cove. They'll make fun of us until the day we die!"

"Speaking of dying," said Brutus as he nervously glanced at the locked door. "How long do you think we can go without food or water?"

"Oh, days and days and days," said Harriet with an airy wave of the hand. "And even then we'll find something to sustain us down here." She glanced at the fungus-covered wall in the more dank part of the basement. "Do you think that's edible? It looks edible."

Brutus shivered. "I don't want to find out, do you?"

"No, maybe not," said Harriet. "Though it looks a lot like that chlorella Odelia likes to eat, or even spirulina, and that's

45

supposed to be very good for you. She says they're super-foods, and superfoods are very beneficial to the health of your gut, Brutus."

Brutus took a hold of his gut. It felt very empty, but even then he wasn't so far gone he was willing to eat mold from the walls. Something told him his gut wouldn't like it.

"And we can always drink our own pee," said Harriet. "I could drink yours and you could drink mine. People have been known to survive that way," she explained. "It was on the Discovery Channel last week."

"I thought you hated the Discovery Channel?" asked Brutus.

"Oh, it's all right. Tex loves to watch it, and Gran does, too, from time to time, and since us cats don't have control over the remote, we're forced to watch with them."

"There must be a way out of here," said Brutus, searching around. "Some secret passageway or hidden door?"

"I'm sorry to have to tell you this, Brutus, but this isn't like the kind of place Nancy Drew or the Hardy Boys always end up in," said Harriet. "No trap doors or secret passage-ways. There's only one way in or out of this basement and that's through that door." Harriet sat down on the cold stone floor and heaved a deep sigh. "We've been had by a mouse, Brutus, and we probably have to learn to accept that horrible truth."

He took up position next to his mate and both sat there for a moment, contemplating what could have been, when suddenly a squeaky voice sounded from right behind them.

"Can I help you with something?"

They both looked in the direction the voice seemed to be coming from, and Harriet was the first one to discover its source.

"Oh, hey, mouse," she said.

"You can call me Molly," said the mouse.

"A member of your family managed to lock us up down here," Harriet explained, "and now we're kinda stuck."

"That will be Rupert," said Molly, a frown on her face, her tiny paws planted on tiny hips. "If I've told him once I've told him a million times: don't mess with the humans or their pets. But does he listen? Of course not. He thinks he's engaged in some sort of noble battle with our mortal enemy or something. Are you our mortal enemy, cats?"

"I guess… we are, in a sense," said Harriet. "'Or at least Odelia sent us down here to get rid of you, so there's something very enemy-like to that."

"Look, we don't want any trouble," said Molly. "And if Rupert has given you trouble, my sincerest apologies. He runs a little wild, my Rupert does."

"Is he…"

"My husband? Yes, he is. And also the father of my four hundred babies."

"Four hundred babies," said Brutus, gulping slightly. "How about that?"

"Four hundred is a lot," Harriet admitted.

"Yeah, they're a handful," Molly agreed.

"Brutus and I can't have babies, you see," said Harriet. "We tried but it turns out our humans had him castrated and had me spayed, so now we can't have kittens."

"We thought about adopting," said Brutus, "but it's such a hassle, with all the paperwork and the home visits and all, so we just figure, why bother, you know?"

"Yeah, I'm not even sure I want to be a mother at this point," said Harriet. "We live a very full and happy life, Brutus and I, along with our dear friends and of course the humans who graciously take care of us. So why have kids, I mean? We might regret the decision and then what?"

"It's not as if we can give them back," said Brutus.

"Well, technically we could," said Harriet.

"You mean…"

"Yeah, we could always tell the adoption agency it didn't work out and then they'll probably find another family to place them with."

"But that's not fair on those kids."

"No, it's not."

"Well, all I can say is that kids are a lot of work," said Molly. "But it's worth it."

"You think?" said Harriet, placing her head on her paws so she was closer to Molly's level. "It's very interesting to hear you say that."

"She hasn't completely given up on her dream," Brutus explained.

"No, I haven't," said Harriet. "Though it took this conversation to realize that."

"Not for me," said Brutus. "I've always known that about you, snookums."

"You have? That's so perceptive of you, my turtle dove."

"You're lucky in that you have a good partner," said Molly. "A good partner is key. If I had to do this all by myself, I wouldn't have done it. But with Rupert it works great."

"Oh, so Rupert is a good father, is he?" said Harriet, surprised to hear that the obnoxious and frankly annoying rodent they'd met had another, softer side to him.

"Oh, yeah, he's great with the kids. Likes to play with them, but can also be strict when he needs to be."

"You have to be strict," said Harriet. "You need to raise them with a firm paw."

"They need to know their limits," Brutus said, nodding.

"I think you'd make a great daddy, buttercup," said Harriet.

"You really think so, honey bug?" he said, touched.

"Yes, I do. I've always thought that."

"Aw, that's so sweet of you to say. I think you'd make a great mother."

"You do? Why, thank you, pookie bear."

"And I think you two would make great parents," said Molly, adding her two cents.

"You know, Molly," said Harriet. "Now that I got to know you a little better, I have to say my entire idea of mice as a species has taken a radical turn for the better."

"I'm glad to hear you say that, Harriet," said Molly. "Likewise. I mean, listening to Rupert it's almost as if cats are the worst creatures on the entire planet, and I always told him, 'Rupert,' I say, 'cats are probably a lot nicer than you think if only you would bother to get to know them a little better.' You know? But does he listen? Of course not. 'Get to know them better!' he'll say. 'Do you want to be eaten? Huh? Do you want to become breakfast, lunch and dinner to a bunch of vicious hairy monsters?'"

"We're not vicious monsters, are we, Brutus?" asked Harriet.

"I don't feel like a vicious monster," said Brutus. "I really don't."

"Live and let live has always been my motto," said Harriet. "There's a place under the sun for every creature on this planet. Isn't that what I always say, Brutus?"

"It is," Brutus confirmed. He couldn't actually remember ever hearing those exact words from his partner's lips, but it did sound like something she could have said.

"I think we should all try to live together in perfect harmony," said Molly now. "That's what I teach my kids, and that's the kind of life I try to live as an example for them."

"Inspiring," said Harriet, nodding. "You're an inspiration, Molly. My hat off to you."

"Likewise," said Brutus, who wondered why Harriet was suddenly talking about non-existent hats. Then again, a large chunk of the conversation had gone right over his head, including but not limited to the virtues Harriet had suddenly extolled of motherhood.

"A quick question, though," said Harriet now.

"Shoot," said Molly. "Anything for my new best friends."

"Could you tell your husband to open the door so we can get out of this basement? He accidentally closed it."

"Oh, you don't need that door," said Molly. "There's plenty of ways in and out. Just follow me."

And with these words she headed to a corner of the basement, Harriet and Brutus right on her heels. The mouse moved beyond an old toboggan, and they followed suit, though they had to displace the object to fit behind it. And then the mouse vanished from view. Harriet and Brutus searched around, but found no trace of her, until her tiny head with the long whiskers came peeping out of a tiny hole at the bottom of the wall.

"Over here," said Molly. "If you follow me I'll lead you straight to the next floor." And then her little head popped off again.

"Um, Molly?" said Harriet.

Molly's head reappeared, her nose twitching as she sniffed the air. "Yah?"

"Um... not to put too fine a point on it, but we're too big to fit in there."

"Nonsense," said Molly. "You'll fit just fine. Just make yourself small."

"But..." said Harriet. "I'm not sure if..."

"Oh, don't be such a pussy," said Molly. "You know what they say, if your head fits, the rest of your body does, too. So just follow me, and you'll be out of here in no time."

"Oh, all right," said Harriet finally, and proceeded to stuff her head into the tiny hole.

And then she was stuck.

She couldn't move forward, in spite of the theory about the fitting head Molly had expounded, and she couldn't move back either, as her head was wedged in too tight.

"Um… Molly?" she said. "You're not going to believe this, but I think I'm stuck."

And then Molly appeared right in front of her nose. Harriet had to squint a little to get a clear view of the mouse, but she was right there, and much to Harriet's surprise the cute little mouse, mother of no less than four hundred baby mice, was smirking at her.

"You stupid cat," she said.

"Pardon me?" said Harriet, shocked by this sudden change in demeanor.

"I got you good, didn't I? Did you really think I'd help you out of this basement? So you could hunt us all down and eat us whole? I know what you cats are like. All sweet talk and surface charm until you pounce on us and gobble us up without batting an eye."

"But-but-but I thought we were friends," said Harriet, shocked at this denouement. "I thought we were kindred spirits."

"Kindred spirits my tush. I'm a mouse and you're a cat, cat, and we will always be mortal enemies, no matter how you look at it."

Just then, Molly was joined by a familiar figure. It was her husband Rupert, who'd slung an arm around his wife's shoulder. "I'm so proud of you, darling," he said. "You trapped the beast!"

"Of course I did. If I had to leave it all up to you she would still be roaming around, probably thinking up ways and means of feeding on my babies."

"Good riddance," Rupert agreed.

"Hey, you have to let me out," said Harriet, getting a little nervous. "I don't like small spaces!"

"Oh, shut up, you whiny pussy," said Molly, nothing like the nice and sweet mouse she'd appeared before. She was a tough little creature, and gave Harriet the evil eye.

"Try to catch us now, cat," said Rupert.

"Yeah, good luck with that," said Molly.

"And now we bid you adieu."

"Adieu. That's French for 'Goodbye and good riddance.'"

"Hey!" said Harriet. "You can't leave me here!"

"Watch us," said Molly, and then both she and her husband disappeared down the hole and all Harriet could hear was the laughter of what sounded like hundreds of mice.

Either it was the echo of Rupert and Molly, or that of their four hundred kids.

Whatever it was, the sound struck Harriet as very unpleasant, but what was even more unpleasant than the stinging ridicule or the fact that she'd gotten her head stuck in a mouse hole, was the sheer indignation of the situation. Now who was the fool?

CHAPTER 8

*V*esta was still thinking about the end of the world, and when it might happen, when the outer office door swung open and Scarlett Canyon walked in from the street.

"Oh, you've got to be kidding me," Vesta muttered, then sat up a little straighter. Scarlett might be her mortal enemy, but she was also an inveterate gossip, and if she found Vesta slumped at her desk, looking less than her best, word would be all over town that she'd been in a terrible state and had probably turned to liquor, just like her late husband had done.

"What do you want?" she asked.

"That's no way to greet one of your patients," said Scarlett, pursing her blowfish lips.

Scarlett probably spent her entire pension on the kind of treatments popularized by Gwyneth Paltrow or Jennifer Aniston, designed to make them stay young forever. At one time even Gran herself had been an avid fan of Goop, and had ordered several items that she'd hoped would clear up her skin and add to her eternal youth, like those bees

Gwyneth was so crazy about, and that you needed to allow to sting you for some reason.

"You're not a patient of mine," said Vesta now.

"Thank God for that," said Scarlett, then laughed a light laugh. "Imagine me, being a patient of yours. That simply wouldn't do, would it?"

"Tell me you're here for a lobotomy and I'll gladly do the honors," Vesta growled.

"I just wanted to make an appointment."

"You could have called."

"I was in the neighborhood."

"Still. Why bother a hard-working woman like me if you could have simply picked up the phone?"

"I thought I'd have a nice little chat with an old best friend." She glanced around and heaved a wistful little sigh. "Do you remember when I used to work here? The waiting room overflowing with patients? The place buzzing with business?" She directed a pointed look at the empty waiting room.

"It's one of our quiet moments," said Vesta. "The lull before the storm."

Scarlett rapped her knuckles on the counter. "I hear they found a skeleton in your basement? One of your old boyfriends? Couldn't hack it anymore and decided to brick himself up inside your wall?"

"Ha ha. Very funny. If your jokes were any funnier I'd bust a gut. Besides, it wasn't a body, it was a skeleton."

"Isn't a skeleton, like, an old body that lost its pep? Like a certain person we know?" She cocked an eyebrow at Vesta, who decided to ignore the slur.

"I'm sure that skeleton has been there forever. From what my daughter told me it's probably been there from when the house was built, way back in the fifties."

"Is that right?" said Scarlett, clearly not believing a word of this. "I'll bet it's that no-good husband of yours. Do you think the police are going to exhume his coffin now? To find out if it's really Jack we buried, or a pile of bricks?"

Vesta directed her most fiery glare at the woman. "How dare you speak of my husband like that?"

"Well, he was my husband as much as he was yours, now, wasn't he? At least in the biblical sense."

She had half a mind to grab the woman's blond hair and give it a good pull, to find out once and for all if it was a wig or her real hair, but restrained herself with a powerful effort. Tex had recently reminded her, after a similar altercation with Scarlett, that she was the public face of this office, and that if she misbehaved it reflected badly on him, and might even put him out of business. She'd argued that, if anything, a fight put bodies in seats, as everybody likes a good scuffle, and none more so than those cheapskate patients of his, who never enjoyed their entertainment more than when it was free of charge. So he should probably give her a pay raise each time she and Scarlett squared off.

Scarlet had casually taken a small black object from her purse and placed it on the counter. "Oh, look at the time," she said. "I have to be going." And then, before Vesta's widening eyes, she folded the object open and the screen suddenly doubled in size.

It was a foldable smartphone—the holy grail of smartphones.

"Where did you get that?" she demanded heatedly.

"Oh, Dick Bernstein gave it to me," said Scarlett.

"No way," said Vesta. "Dick gave one to me."

"I know! But you broke it, didn't you?" She held up the nifty little gadget and tapped at the screen with her freakishly long fake nails. "So lucky for him he was fully insured, so he bought himself another one."

"And then gave it to you? Has he lost his mind?"

Scarlett shrugged. "He knows I'm more careful with his gifts than you are."

"Can I help it if he gave me a lemon?"

"The story he told me was that you dropped it in the soup."

"It broke first. I only dumped it in the soup to put out the fire."

"A likely story," said Scarlett with a little laugh, and once again Vesta had to suppress a strong inclination to put her hands around the woman's neck and squeeze. "At least he gifted me this phone. He only loaned you his, before you decided to dunk it in your soup."

"I'm telling you, it broke and caught fire!"

"Yes, well, I guess that's your story and you'll stick to it, won't you? But Dick was pretty cross, Vesta. He said he's never coming near you again. And I can't blame him. First you go and destroy his nice new phone, and then the police start finding dead bodies in your basement, so… Well, I must be off now. Give my love to Tex, will you?"

"Didn't you need to make an appointment about something? Those hemorrhoids of yours, for instance?"

Shocked, Scarlett glared at her. "I don't have hemorrhoids."

"You don't? So maybe one of your fake boobs sprang a leak?"

Scarlett's lips drew together into a thin line, which was an amazing feat, given the fact that they were stuffed to the gills with collagen. "One day, Vesta, something really nasty will happen to you. Something that's gonna knock that mean streak you got right out of you. And when it does, you'll need a friend, and you'll be sad to discover you don't have any friends. You managed to scare them all away with that forked tongue of yours."

"Oh, just buzz off, will you? And tell Dick his phone is a piece of junk."

"I will tell him no such thing. And when we've been going steady for a month, and he gifts me a diamond necklace, I'll tell him he's much better off with me than he ever was with you. If he'd stayed with you he probably would have found himself murdered and stuffed down your basement, and that skeleton they found is living proof I'm right."

And with this powerful harangue she was finally off, slamming the door as she went.

"Skeleton... living proof," Gran muttered with a grin as she wrote down the gist of the conversation. She'd been keeping a diary for a while now, all colorful stories about the colorful people that inhabited this colorful town of hers. Odelia often borrowed from her observations for her pieces in the *Gazette*. She could have used a note-taking app on her phone, of course, but with the NSA spying on every phone in existence, she didn't need her deepest darkest secrets being salivated over by some government pencil pusher.

Having preserved Scarlett's words for posterity, she picked up her phone and called her daughter. Marge picked up at the first ring. "So who the hell is that dead body?"

CHAPTER 9

*M*arge was hanging up the laundry in the backyard when her phone demanded her attention. She picked it out of her apron pocket and pressed the red Connect button. "Yes, Ma?" she said dutifully.

"So who the hell is that dead body in your basement?"

"My basement? Our basement, you mean."

"Not when there's dead bodies. Then it's your basement. So who is it?"

"We don't know yet. Abe was here and took the body and he'll run some tests."

"What tests? To make sure it's really dead? Abe is losing it, honey."

"Not to see if it's dead. To figure out who it is."

"Well, it's not your father, that much I can tell you."

"Of course it's not my father. I know that much."

"And don't you forget it, oh, daughter of mine."

Marge's expression softened. "Have people been saying things?"

"If with people you mean Scarlett Canyon then yes,

they've been saying I killed my husband and dumped his body in the basement."

"That's impossible. That skeleton has been there for many, many years. Probably way before we bought the house." She suppressed a shiver. "Can you imagine we lived in that house all these years with a dead person in the basement? I must have passed that spot hundreds of times, without knowing there was a dead person buried there. It's simply too horrible to contemplate."

"Then don't. What does Alec say?"

"He's very upset, too. Especially since Abe will need a lot of time to figure this out."

"Weren't there any clothes, a watch, a wallet or something?"

"There are remnants of clothes. Rags, really. Abe thinks it's a man, judging from the bone structure. Oh, and he found a brooch, so that tells me it might be a woman."

"Or a dude wearing a brooch," said Vesta. "Was it a nice brooch?"

"A very nice brooch. Looks very expensive. At least if those diamonds are real, of course. They could be zirconium, though I don't think so. They looked real to me."

"So did you pocket the brooch?"

"No, of course not. Why would I pocket the brooch?"

"To sell it, of course. If it's as valuable as you say it is, it might net us a small fortune."

"God, Ma. I'm not even deigning that obscene suggestion with a response."

"So how about the leak? At least tell me Gwayn plugged the leak."

"No, he didn't. And he's not allowed to go anywhere near that basement because Alec turned it into a crime scene. So until he decides otherwise…"

"No water."

"No water," said Marge miserably. "I had to use Odelia's machine to do the laundry, and I guess we'll have to go over there for our showers and meals, too. In fact we might as well move in with her and Chase, as I don't feel comfortable staying here as long as that body is still downstairs."

"Why? It's been there all this time and you were never bothered."

"That's because I didn't know it was there, Ma."

"Anyway, I just called to tell you that I'm going to be needing that basement from now on. At least once that dead carcass is carted out of there."

"You're going to need the basement? Why? What are you planning to do with it?"

"Turning it into a bunker, of course, what else?"

Marge closed her eyes. This was too much. First the water thing, then the skeleton, and now her mother was going nuts on her again. "Listen, Ma. I can't deal with this right now, so whatever you've got in mind, please don't tell me, all right?"

"Sure, fine. Be that way. It's your funeral." And with these words, the old lady disconnected.

"My funeral indeed," Marge muttered as she tucked away her phone. A voice sounding nearby had her jump about a foot in the air.

"So a dead body, huh? How about that?"

It was Marcie from next door. Marge moved to the hedge dividing the two backyards and gave up a sigh of exasperation. "It's been one hell of a morning, Marcie, let me tell you that."

"I'll bet it has. First the water thing and now this body, huh?"

Marcie and Ted had been Marge and Tex's neighbors for twenty-five years. In fact both couples had moved into their respective homes around the same time, and had become firm friends and friendly neighbors ever since. Not that they dropped in on each other all the time, but they had regular chats over the dividing hedge, just like now.

"So do they know who it is?" asked Marcie. She was a dark-haired woman, going a little gray now, with a stern face and a deep groove between her brows that looked as if it had been cut with a knife. She had a slim figure Marge had always envied, even though she was quite slender herself.

"No idea," said Marge. "Though I have a feeling it could have been there for decades."

"The first thing Ted told me was that Vesta must have dumped one of her old boyfriends down there." She laughed, but Marge wasn't laughing along.

"Is that what people are saying?"

"No, well, yes, probably. But you know I don't take any of that stuff seriously, right?"

Marge nodded. She could probably expect some curious glances when she went grocery shopping. "Do you remember the Bakers?" she asked.

"Phyllis, yes. Her husband? I don't think so. We moved in a couple of months after you and Tex did, remember? The only people I remember are the Coopers, though we only met once. They'd moved out before we took our first look at the house. We mainly dealt with the realtor at the time."

"Well, the husband wasn't in the picture when we moved in. I remember Phyllis very well, though, and her daughter, of course. Rita Baker was Odelia's babysitter for years."

"Oh, of course. She moved into an apartment on Grover Street, didn't she?"

"She did. And was so wonderful to knock ten percent off the price when Odelia bought the house. She had a brother, too, though we never saw much of him."

Rita's mother Phyllis had moved into a nursing home twenty-five years ago, but Rita had stayed in the house next door until five years before, when she decided the house was too big for her, and had bought an apartment. Odelia had jumped at the chance to move in next to her parents, and Marge and Tex helped her out with the down payment.

"Funny, though, right?" said Marcie now.

"What is?"

"Well, first the Bakers lived here, with their daughter living next door, and now you and Tex live here, with Odelia where Rita used to live. Almost as if history repeats itself."

"Yeah, I guess in a way that's true," Marge agreed, though she didn't really want to think of herself as an old lady being forced to move into a nursing home just yet.

"Whatever happened to Phyllis Baker?" asked Marcie now, leaning on the hedge.

"She passed away. About ten years ago, I guess."

"What about her husband?"

"We never met. As I remember it, Rita once told me he walked out on them. But this must have happened when Rita herself was quite young, her brother still in his teens."

They shared a look of significance. "We may just have figured out that skeleton's identity, Marge," said Marcie.

"Yes, we may have done just that," said Marge.

Marcie gave her a sympathetic nod. "If you need anything, just give a holler."

"Thanks, Marcie. That means a lot."

And as she moved back to her laundry and hung up one of Tex's checked shirts, her mind kept going back to the mystery of Mr. Baker, and whether he might be the skeleton in her basement. Somehow she doubted it. Phyllis Baker hadn't been a murderer, and Rita and Tom definitely weren't. Still, it was all very intriguing.

CHAPTER 10

*D*ooley and I had arrived in Morley Street, the place where, according to Kingman at least, and I had no reason to doubt him, as Kingman is usually one of the best-informed cats in town, the oldest animal in Hampton Cove lived.

"So what is a macaw, Max?" asked Dooley.

"I think it's a kind of parrot," I said. "One with very colorful plumage, too. It's also an endangered species, as humans tend to catch them in the wild and sell them as pets."

"Is that what happened to us? Did someone catch us in the wild and sell us?"

Dooley has a tendency to ask tough questions from time to time, and I guess now was such a time. "I don't think so, Dooley. I don't think we ever lived in the wild. Or at least I can't remember that I did."

"Me neither," he admitted.

"I seem to remember Odelia telling us she got us straight from our mothers," I said. "And that doesn't sound very wild to me."

"Straight from our mothers," Dooley echoed, and already

I could see the wheels turning in his head. "So… who was my mother, Max? And my father?"

"No idea, Dooley. You'd have to ask Odelia. Or Gran."

"I will," he said.

We'd been wandering up and down the street, wondering where to find this old bird, when suddenly I was struck with an idea. Yes, it happens.

"We're going about this all wrong, Dooley."

"We are?"

"Yes, where do birds live?"

"In the trees?"

"Apart from the trees."

"Um… in cages?"

"Unfortunately, yes, but also in backyards. So why don't we go from backyard to backyard and try to find this bird that way?" I suggested.

And now that we had a plan of campaign, we decided to put it into action immediately. So we moved between two houses, where a narrow strip of lawn divided both structures, and arrived in the backyard of what looked like a very ordinary house, not unlike our own. Looking here and there, we kept an eye out for our colorful feathered friend, hoping we'd find her soon and she would be able to enlighten us.

"Have you noticed how all these houses look exactly the same, Max?" asked Dooley as we traversed one backyard and then moved into the next.

He was right. It was almost as if we were home, even though we weren't. There were backyards that had swings and plastic toys for kids, and others that had lawn chairs out where people could snooze, while still others had small pools installed, or even fish ponds where colorful fish swam. It all looked very suburban and very cozy to me.

"I think it's because humans all like the same thing," I said.

"What is that?"

"Whatever the neighbors have. If the neighbor has a pool, they want the bigger pool. If their neighbor has a new car, they also want one, only bigger and flashier and more expensive. The human mind is a parrot, Dooley. A mimicking machine."

"Like Camilla."

"Like Camilla."

"So if Odelia has a cat, her neighbor also wants a cat, only bigger and better?"

"Um… well, maybe this parrot thing doesn't apply to cats," I allowed. Odelia's neighbor Kurt Mayfield hates cats, for some reason, and each time we hold one of our impromptu rehearsals in the backyard likes to show his lack of appreciation by throwing shoes in our direction, and not because he likes us so much and ran out of bouquets.

We'd arrived in a backyard where the owner had added a nice verandah to the house, with a lot of nice-looking flowers blooming inside the structure. It all looked very colorful, and reminded me of the rainforest, or what little I'd seen of it on TV.

"There!" Dooley suddenly cried, and pointed with his paw in the direction of the verandah.

I glanced over, and discovered he was right. What initially I'd taken for another flower turned out to be a very large bird of colorful plumage instead. It had red plumes, but also green ones and blue ones and yellow ones. As if a kid had been given a box of crayons and told to draw the most vivid and most colorful bird imaginable.

We moved closer to the house, and I saw that a window in the verandah was ajar, so we hopped up onto the garden table and I put my face against the crack. "Hey, there," I said by way of introduction. "Is your name by any chance Camilla?"

The parrot slowly turned in my direction, a visible frown on her face. "Who's asking?"

"I'm Max," I said. "And I would like to have a word with you, Mrs. Parrot."

"I'm not a parrot," said the parrot. "I'm a macaw."

"Sorry, Mrs. Macaw."

"Who's that scrawny mongrel next to you, big cat?" asked the macaw.

"That's Dooley. He's my friend and also a detective, just like me."

"A detective, eh? Now that's a first. Most cats I know are hunters. Killers."

"We're not that kind of cats," I assured her. "In fact I can't even remember the last time I did any hunting. Or killing, for that matter."

"No, I guess you prefer your meals straight from the can or aluminum pouch."

"Exactly," I said. "So the thing is, we would like to pick your brain, Mrs. Macaw."

"You want to do what with my brain?" asked the parrot—or macaw.

"Pick it," I said. "You know, like, pick your brain."

"I knew it. Stay away from me, cat. And don't come anywhere near my brain. I like my brain just the way it is, and don't want it picked to pieces, if it's all the same to you."

"No, it's just an expression," I said. "All we want to do is ask you a couple of questions, that's all. There will be no picking of brains going on. No brain business whatsoever."

"She thinks we're Hannibal Lecter, Max," said Dooley, seated beside me and following the conversation with rapt attention. "She thinks we like to eat brains."

"We do not want to eat your brain," I said, just to make my meaning perfectly clear. "No brain will be eaten in the course of this interview. We just want to, um, consult it."

"Download it," Dooley added.

"She doesn't know what downloading is, Dooley. She's obviously very, very old, and probably has never even seen a computer."

"Oh, I've seen a computer," said the big parrot. "I even use it from time to time. If you stay right there and don't come any closer, I'll show you." The parrot moved over to a round-shaped device that stood in the corner of the verandah, and cleared her throat for a moment, then spoke into it, enunciating very clearly, "Alexa, are cats dangerous?"

The device immediately answered, "Cats are predators and prey on birds and small mammals. It is estimated that the seventy-six million cats in the United States hunt and kill billions of animals annually. My advice? Steer clear if you're a bird or a mammal."

"Thanks, Alexa," said the parrot gratefully. "I will."

"Hey, that's pretty cool," I said.

"What is it, Max?" asked Dooley, who couldn't see very well, since the window was a little steamed up because of all the plants inside the verandah—a regular rainforest.

"Here, take my place," I said, and switched places with him.

"You want another demonstration? Fine? Watch this, cat," said the parrot. "Alexa, who is the most lethal pet in existence?"

"The cat is the most vicious pet in existence."

"That's not very nice," said Dooley.

"Yeah, I'm sure that's not true," I said. "What about snakes and spiders and scorpions?"

"I specifically asked most vicious *pet*," said Camilla.

"Snakes and spiders and scorpions are pets," I said. "At least to some people."

"Can you please stop leering at me, cat?" asked Camilla. "And salivating?"

"I'm not leering, though," said Dooley. "I'm just trying to figure out if the skeleton in our human's basement belongs to someone who used to live there. That's all. I don't want to leer at you, Mrs. Parrot. Or salivate, whatever salivate means."

"It means you want to eat her so much saliva is dripping from your mouth," I said.

"No, it's not," said Dooley, and licked his lips just to be sure. "Is it?"

"Look, Mrs. Macaw—" I began.

"Call me Camilla," said the macaw, a first indication she was not as anti-cat as we thought.

"I'm Dooley," said Dooley, "and this Is Max."

"Yes, you told me before," said Camilla. "So you want to know about a skeleton you buried in the basement of your human's house, is that it? Probably a mouse or a rat, or even a bird like me. Cats don't mind leaving behind the evidence of their villainy."

"It's a human skeleton, actually," I said, putting my face into the window again.

"A human skeleton? Well, you've outdone yourselves this time, haven't you?"

"We didn't kill it," I said. "It wasn't us."

"Alexa," she said, turning to the device once more. "Do cats eat humans?"

"Only very rarely do cats feast on human flesh," this Alexa machine spoke in its weirdly mellifluous voice, "and usually only if that human is dead already."

"Thanks, Alexa," said Camilla cheerfully. "See? You probably killed this human and don't even remember. That's cats for you. They are such prolific killers they don't even remember their last kill."

"Um, we don't eat humans, though," I said. Just the thought. Yuck.

"Mostly we eat Purina," said Dooley.

"Purina? That's an animal I'm not familiar with," said Camilla. "Alexa, who's Purina?"

"Purina is a brand of pet food," said Alexa.

"Oh, of course. Now I see. So you killed this human, then had Purina for dessert."

"Look, cats didn't kill this human," I said, slowly this time. "Another human either killed this human and buried the body, or they died of natural causes and for some reason someone—not a cat—decided it was a good idea to bury them in our basement."

"I see," said the parrot, frowning. "So are you quite sure cats didn't do it?"

"Yes, I'm one hundred percent sure. One thousand percent."

"Cats are devious. So how do I know you're not lying to me? How do I know you're not simply distracting me while other, even bigger cats than yourself are sneaking up on me right now, ready to strike!" And to indicate she was considering this a likely contingency, suddenly she turned around and yelled, "Better show yourself, cats!"

"I'm right here," said Dooley.

But Camilla kept scanning her surroundings, searching for those elusive hunting cats.

"I have a feeling we're not going to get a lot out of this old bird, Max," said Dooley.

"I have the same feeling," I said.

"So you don't remember a human going missing in Harrington Street several decades ago?" I asked, deciding to give this one final try.

"Alexa," said the parrot in response, "do cats hunt like velociraptors, meaning one cat keeps its prey busy and distracted while two other cats sneak up on it and flank it?"

"Cats are solitary hunters," Alexa intoned cheerfully. "They do not hunt in packs."

"Thanks, Alexa," said the bird, turning back to face us. "What were you saying?"

"I think we'll be on our way, Mrs. Macaw," said Dooley.

"Yes, we're very sorry to have troubled you, Camilla," I added.

"Is this a trick question?" asked the parrot, narrowing her eyes.

Instead of responding to what I frankly considered a rude question, I heaved my paw in a gesture of goodbye, and then we were off, leaving the paranoid bird to her no doubt very inspiring and lively conversations with this Alexa thing.

"Poor parrot," said Dooley. "She seems to have a lot of weird ideas about cats."

"Yeah, she really hates us," I agreed. "Hates our guts big time."

"Too bad. She could have told us a great deal about the things she knows."

We were quiet as we traipsed through the backyards on our way back to the street. So far our investigation was a bust. But I still held hope we would be useful to Odelia some way soon. Not by hunting mice, or by interviewing the oldest living pet in Hampton Cove. And as we made our way back through the backyards suddenly a man threw a shoe at me and yelled, "Get out of here, you vermin!"

"Is it just me, or are we not very welcome in this part of Hampton cove, Dooley?"

"It's not just you, Max," he said, as a second shoe hit my back.

So we both went off at a trot, glad to leave these dangerous backyards behind.

"Let's go home," I said. Frankly I'd had enough for one day.

"I'm hungry," Dooley intimated, and I had to admit I shared his sentiments exactly.

At least Odelia would never throw shoes at us, or ask Alexa a series of very insulting and insinuating questions.

"Maybe by now Odelia already knows who that skeleton belongs to," said Dooley. "And maybe she already knows who killed it, too."

I perked up at that. "I'll bet you're right."

We may be pet detectives—or detecting pets—but that doesn't mean we're always raring to go. Sometimes we simply want to curl up into a ball and have a nice nap, and let the world pass us by, with its skeletons, annoying parrots and shoe-throwing humans.

CHAPTER 11

*O*delia was at the office of the *Gazette,* talking to her editor. She'd flung herself down on the leather couch he kept in his office for visitors, and was staring up at the ceiling while Dan had gone in search of something in the *Gazette's* archives. The skeleton had carefully been exhumed by the county coroner's people and shipped off to the lab for examination. As soon as they knew more they'd call Alec. Meanwhile Odelia, who wasn't accustomed to waiting around, decided to dig a little deeper into the history of the house her parents inhabited, and come up with a clue to the dead person's identity that way.

"Here we are," said Dan as he returned, carrying a thick book with bundled old copies of the newspaper he'd founded.

"Shouldn't you digitize the entire archive, Dan?" asked Odelia not for the first time.

"Yes, I probably should," he said. "And maybe once I retire I will. But for now I have too much work putting out fresh copies each and every week and so do you, my dear."

He placed the thick collection on top of the pile of papers on his desk.

Odelia had gotten up and frowned as she stared at what looked like a copy of the *Gazette* from the stone ages, judging from the quality of the paper, yellowed and old.

"What am I looking at?" she asked, her eyes drawn to an article about the biggest pumpkin ever to be harvested in Hampton Cove history.

"This," said Dan, tapping a finger on an article in the bottom right corner.

'Local Man Missing,' the headline read. As she scanned through the article, her excitement grew with leaps and bounds. "Boyd Baker—Harrington Street 46. That's him!"

"I thought so," said Dan with a grin. "I keep a list of Missing Persons, and there he was, our Mr. Boyd Baker, disappeared exactly fifty-five years ago."

Odelia quickly read through the article. Boyd Baker had worked for Courtyard Living, a local landscaping company, and hadn't returned home from work one day. His wife Phyllis had reported him missing, and the police vowed they'd do everything to find him.

"I remember Boyd Baker," said Dan. "Even though I was only a kid back then."

"A kid who published a newspaper."

"Well, yes, I did," he said modestly.

"So what was he like, this Boyd Baker?"

"A big man. Very impressive. Though I mainly remember his wife Phyllis. She worked at the pharmacy. Very sweet woman. And Rita, of course. She was quite the stunner. Too old for me, of course, but a boy can dream." A little color had seeped into his cheeks.

"She used to babysit me," said Odelia. "The ideal babysitter, too. I loved our evenings."

"I wish she'd been my babysitter."

Odelia smiled. "I take it nothing ever happened between you and Rita Baker?"

"Nope. That's the way it goes with these boyhood crushes."

"I wonder what happened to Phyllis Baker. When my parents bought the house it was because she was moving into a nursing home. She was eighty and this was twenty-five years ago. So she would now be…"

"Not among us anymore, I guess."

"No, probably not. Though Rita will still be alive, and her brother. I bought the house on Harrington Street five years ago, and Rita even helped me with the move, so…"

"I still see Rita from time to time. She lives in one of those new apartments on Grover Street now. She's your grandma's age."

"You're no spring chicken yourself, Dan," said Odelia with a grin.

"Don't remind me, young lady. You know what they say: you're only as old as you feel, and I still feel a fit fifteen most of the time, a dirty thirty on my bad days."

"I didn't know you had bad days."

"I try to skip over them."

She studied the picture of the man in whose house her parents now lived, and thought he looked bluff and hearty, with a mischievous twinkle in his eye. She didn't remember Rita ever talking about her dad much. Time to have a little chat now.

"I think it's him," she said finally. "I think this is the man we found in the basement."

"If that's your first instinct, he's your guy. You know what I've always told you."

"Always to follow my hunches." And to Dan's credit, he was right. Odelia's hunches often led her in the right direction, even if at first they seemed outrageous or even crazy.

"Oh, before I forget," said Dan. "This story about the skeleton being your grandfather. Town gossip?"

"What? Of course town gossip. Grandpa died of a heart attack, and is buried in Saint-John's cemetery." She stared at her editor, who pursed his lips. "I don't believe this."

"Well, you know what this town is like, Odelia. Tongues are wagging so fast it's a miracle no sprains have been reported yet."

"So that's the consensus? That because my grandmother lives in that house it has to be her late husband?"

"Whom she killed with an ax and then buried in the basement. Yeah, that seems to be the gist. Five people already stopped me in the street to tell me all about it."

"Gran didn't even live on Harrington Street at the time. Mom and Dad only moved there twenty-five years ago, right before I was born, and Gran didn't even move in with them until years later. Gran and Grandpa lived in the house on Hay Mill, and when Gran kicked him out he moved to Munster Street, which is where he died. From a heart attack. People know this, Dan, so why are they telling these crazy stories?"

"Because they can? Because it makes them feel important? Oh, I'm sure this will all blow over. As soon as the police confirm it's Boyd Baker the rumors will go away."

"I hope so. Gran doesn't deserve to be subjected to this kind of nonsense."

"Then you better go and talk to Rita Baker and ask her about her father." He wiggled his eyebrows. "And tell her Dan Goory said hi, will you?"

She laughed. "Oh, Dan."

"What? A boyhood crush never fades, Odelia. It only becomes sweeter with time."

CHAPTER 12

*C*hase was in his office when his boss popped his head in the door. "Abe just called, buddy. He thinks he's got something," said the Chief, sounding and looking excited.

Immediately Chase shot up from behind his desk and followed his superior officer into his office. The phone was on speaker. "Go for Chase and Alec, Abe," said the Chief.

"Chase and Alec. Sounds like a comedy double act," Abe quipped, then turned serious. "I've checked dental records, which at this point is all I have to go on, and I just got a hit. It would appear that our John Doe is a Mr. Boyd Baker, who used to reside at the address where his remains were found. Also, and this is preliminary, so don't quote me on it, I think I've nailed down the cause of death. Our late Mr. Baker has a very large hole where part of his skull used to be. It's entirely consistent with a blow to the head with a blunt object. He must have been knocked out with such force he either died on the spot, or died as a consequence of the blow. Mind you, this is all basically conjecture on my part. There's really no way for me to know with absolute certainty what the man died of."

"Anything else?" asked Chief Alec, his eyes sparkling with excitement.

"The brooch. I've examined it more closely and those are real diamonds. So it's worth a pretty penny. My advice would be to show it to a jeweler. Every jeweler has their personal style, so maybe they'll be able to deduce something from the way the stones were set. There's also a small engraving that had become invisible because of dirt."

"And? What does it say?" asked Chase, hanging on the coroner's every word.

"Some code, so not very helpful. I will send you my preliminary report, and detailed photographs of the brooch. Good luck, gentlemen. And if you have another case like this, please don't hesitate to call me. It's always fun to dig around in the past, instead of the endless number of traffic accident victims I usually deal with."

Chief Alec checked his emails, and sure enough Abe's email had already arrived in his inbox. He clicked on the pictures of the brooch, and both men studied them. The inscription on the back was clearly visible. It read AC/34.

"Doesn't say much," said Chase, disappointed.

"It might mean something to a jeweler," Alec pointed out.

"Did you know this Boyd Baker?" asked Chase.

"I did. Well, not personally. The guy disappeared years ago. But him and his wife lived in that house, all right. In fact Marge and Tex bought the place from Phyllis Baker twenty-five years ago, and even back then the disappearance of her husband was common knowledge. Rumor had it he left town with a girlfriend, leaving his family in the lurch."

"Is Mrs. Baker still with us?"

"No, I don't think so. She was an old lady twenty-five

years ago. But her daughter is still alive. She lived next to her mother, and sold the house to Odelia only five years ago or something. I think she moved to Grover Street, to one of those new apartments."

"So she's our first port of call?"

"That's right, buddy. Oh, and Chase?"

"Mh?"

"Let's keep Odelia out of this one, and my mother."

"No civilian consultants?"

"No civilian consultants. People are already speculating that it's my dad whose skeleton we found, and that my mother murdered him and buried him there. So if we let her and Odelia investigate, the gossip mill will go full tilt. They'll say we're trying to cover up a murder and yadda yadda yadda. Heck, they'll probably say I'm trying to cover up the murder of my dad, but at least I've got the badge to make them shut up."

Chase nodded as he studied the other pictures of the brooch, then focused on the ones Abe had taken of the skeleton as it lay spread out on his autopsy table.

"Amazing," he said softly as he studied the pictures.

"What is?"

"So this guy has been in the ground for decades? Talk about a cold case."

"The coldest one possible," said Alec. "And we're going to solve it, buddy. You and me."

"Are you sure it's a good idea not to involve Odelia? Her cats might be able to—"

"No cat lives for decades," the Chief interrupted him. "So I don't see how Max and the others could help us solve Baker's murder. No, it's just us, Chase. Just like the old days."

Chase laughed. "The old days? Chief, I've only been in town a year."

"Funny," said Alec with a frown. "Sometimes I have a feeling you've been here forever."

&

"I'm bored, Jerry," said Johnny as he leaned his head back. Spot sat in his lap and seemed bored, too, for he had placed his head on Johnny's knee and was panting softly.

"Yeah, well, that's what surveillance is all about," said Jerry.

"Being bored?"

"Stalking out a place until you're ready to move in and rob its owners blind."

"We don't even know if there's anything of value to be found in there, Jer."

"Doesn't matter! This is our trial run, Johnny. This is where we find out how vigilant the cops in this town are, and if this all turns out the way I think it will, we can launch a run that will sustain us for the rest of our lives. Do you realize how much wealth there is in this town? This place is crawling with millionaires and billionaires and gazillionaires."

"All with very sophisticated security systems."

"Which you won't have a problem to hack into."

Johnny perked up. He liked a challenge, and cracking and hacking security systems was his forte. Call it a hobby.

"I don't know, Jer," he said, his smile fading. "I have a bad feeling in my gut. And so does Spot."

"How can you possibly know what feeling Spot has in his tiny little gut? I don't even know if dogs are capable of having feelings in their gut."

"A dog person knows, Jer. And I can feel that he's restless."

"He's probably hungry."

A rumbling sound echoed through the car. Johnny produced a sheepish grin.

"Patience, Johnny, patience. As soon as the house is quiet we go in and do what we do best."

"Raid the fridge?"

"Rob the poor suckers."

CHAPTER 13

We'd finally arrived home and found that the sliding glass door that leads into the living room was closed and locked, which probably meant Odelia had gone out.

"If you're hungry I can always bring you some food, Max," Dooley offered graciously.

"No, it's fine," I said. "I should probably lose some weight, if I ever want to fit through that flap again."

We moved over to Marge and Tex's backyard and discovered the door to the living room was closed there, too, so we hopped up on the porch swing, and moments later were fast asleep. I don't know what awoke me, but it may have been the pitter-patter of raindrops on the porch roof. And as I opened my eyes to take a look, I saw that yes, indeed, the nice sun that had warmed the world had been rudely obscured by a thick deck of clouds, and rain was now pouring from the heavens, soaking all and sundry.

"Good thing we're up here, nice and dry," I said.

"Yes, good thing," Dooley agreed, though he was shivering. With the rain a distinct chill had set in, and Dooley felt it more keenly than I did. He has less insulation from the elements, you see. I have thicker skin, I guess, and perhaps a thicker coat of fur, too.

"You go inside, Dooley," I said. "You don't have to stay out here and catch a cold on my account."

"No, I want to stay with you, Max," he said.

"Please go in. If you catch a cold I'll feel bad."

"Oh, all right."

He trotted off in the direction of the pet flap, and moments later had disappeared inside. And then it was just me and the elements. I wasn't cold, but I still felt the chill. Not sure if it was the weather or the knowledge that beneath my paws, in the basement of the house, a dead man had spent the last couple of decades cooling his or her heels.

Weird thought, I thought, and then promptly dozed off again.

The next thing that awakened me was the movement of the swing. I looked up and saw that Dooley had joined me once more.

"Dooley, I told you to go inside."

"I can't be in there, Max. It's the dead person." He shivered, and this time it wasn't from the cold. "I keep thinking about that skeleton, and how maybe there's a lot of other skeletons buried down there."

"I think there's a big chance this is the only skeleton."

"But how can you be sure? How can you be sure there's not a dozen skeletons buried down there, or underneath the house? Do you remember that movie we saw about the house that had been built on top of an ancient burial ground for Native Americans?"

I distinctly remembered that movie, and was now shivering myself. Odelia loves to watch horror movies, even though they scare her to death, and she always makes us watch them with her, because if she watches them by herself she's too scared to go to bed afterward. Over the years we must have seen dozens of horror movies, and since I don't like horror movies, and neither does Dooley, I remember practically all of them.

And one that stood out to me was one where the heroine of the story at a certain point is trying to stay afloat in a hole where her house used to be, skeletons popping up all around her. It was a horrible scene, and one I remembered with distinct distaste.

"What if the ground is full of skeletons?" Dooley said, "and on a rainy day like this they all come popping up out of the soggy earth and try to drag us down with them?"

"Skeletons don't drag anyone down, Dooley," I pointed out with iron logic. "They're dead, you see, so they don't have the capacity to drag anyone down, and definitely not the two of us."

"In the movie they all came alive again, and tried to drown that poor girl."

"That's because that was just a movie," I said. "And you know that what happens in movies isn't real, Dooley. It's all special effects and make-believe."

"Still," he said as he directed a nervous look at the now soggy lawn, fully expecting the first skeleton to come popping out any moment now, ready to drag us down with it.

"Look, I'm pretty sure that skeleton was the only skeleton buried down there."

"I don't know, Max. This could be an old burial ground of Native Americans. And you know what that means. These dead people get very upset when someone builds a house on top of them, and when they get upset they sink the house and all of its inhabitants."

I swallowed away a lump of uneasiness. Dooley made a good point. "Maybe we should move next door," I suggested.

"I'm sure Odelia's house isn't built on an ancient burial ground."

"Who knows? Maybe this entire neighborhood is built on an ancient burial ground, and we're all in mortal danger."

"In that case we'll make a run for it," I said. "But until the first skeleton pops its head out of the ground, I'm staying put."

And as I tried to go back to sleep, it irked me a little bit that every time I opened my eyes, Dooley was staring intently at the ground, waiting for the first skeleton to appear.

arge arrived at the library just when the first fat drops of rain started pummeling the world below. She hurried inside, and was glad to be out of the rain. Odd, she thought. She checked her weather.com app every morning and also at night before going to bed, and it hadn't mentioned rain for Hampton Cove or the surrounding towns. But then weather prediction wasn't an exact science, and it was notoriously hard to know what surprises the weather gods had in store for mere mortals like her.

And she'd just hung up her coat and moved to the shelf where returns were delivered to start collecting them on a trolley, when the first visitor walked in. It was old Mrs. Samson from down the road. Mrs. Samson, a frequent visitor of the library, loved romance novels—the saucier the better —and faithfully dropped by every week to stock up on a fresh selection of reading material.

"Marge," she said by way of greeting as she ventured into the library, then suddenly turned back. "I just want you to know that I don't believe a word of what people are saying. Not a single word."

"And what are people saying?" asked Marge, though she had a pretty good idea by now.

"Oh, just this and that. About that skeleton, I mean. I've known Vesta for years and years and years and even if she did kill your father I'm sure she must have had her reasons and has never killed again. And if anyone says otherwise I'm putting them straight and telling them that as a dear friend of the family I know, and they don't."

"Thanks, Mrs. Samson," said Marge. Even though Mrs. Samson wasn't exactly a friend of the family it was still touching she was prepared to jump to their defense like that.

"I mean, there are so many violent men out there, and I, for one, don't blame the women who kill them. It's self-defense, isn't it? And with the law being on the side of the perpetrators, a woman has to take the law into her own hands or else she doesn't know what will happen. That man might as well kill her one day if she doesn't kill him first."

"Mrs. Samson, I can assure you that my mother never killed anyone. When my dad died they had been divorced for many years, and it wasn't my mom that killed him but a heart attack."

"Uh-huh," said Mrs. Samson, though it was obvious she didn't believe a word Marge was saying. "Just look at that poor Nicole Kidman in that *Big Fat Lies* series."

"*Big Little Lies*," Marge corrected her.

"That's what I said. Nicole bravely pushed her husband down the stairs because she had to, otherwise that horrible pig would have bashed her head in. Oh, yes, he would have, no matter what Meryl Streep has to say about it."

"First of all, Nicole Kidman didn't push her husband down the stairs," said Marge. "And secondly, like I said, my parents were long divorced before my dad died. And also, my parents never lived in the house on Harrington Street. Tex and I only moved in there twenty-five years ago, and Mom only moved in with us ten years ago, when she felt the house where she was living had become too big for her and so she sold it. So you see, that body in the basement can't possibly be connected to us. That body has been there from way, way before we ever moved in."

"Uh-huh," said Mrs. Samson, then placed a kindly hand on Marge's cheek. "It's so sweet of you to defend your mother like that. I just wish my son would come to my defense more often." She retracted the hand, then said, chipper, "Tell Vesta that I'm on her side. Us women have to stick together, like just like those women in *Fat Big Lies* do."

And she pottered off in the direction of the romance section, to load up on a fresh collection of bodice rippers.

Marge watched her totter off with a shake of the head. If the whole town was thinking what Mrs. Samson was thinking, they were about to face some difficult times.

❧

Odelia arrived at the apartment complex on Grover Street and parked her car across the road. It was a nice new building, in beige brick, and it looked really modern, the way only new apartment blocks can look. There were six apartments, with balconies both front and back, one of which was Rita Baker's. She stepped up to the front door and entered, already practicing her opening statement. She searched the name on the bell.

"Yes?" a melodious voice called out.

"Hi, my name is Odelia Poole. You probably remember me. I bought your house."

"Oh, of course! Come in, Odelia." And immediately the buzzer buzzed and Odelia hurried to push open the door.

Moments later she was mounting the stairs and when she arrived on the second-floor landing, Rita was already there, greeting her with a smile and open arms.

She looked exactly like Odelia remembered: a lady in her seventies, with a lot of soft white curls, and a kindly pink face. She looked a little older, her face a little more lined, but otherwise still the same kindhearted woman. Odelia had bought the house directly from Rita, without the intervention of a broker, which Rita had said she despised for the exorbitant commissions they extracted, and the way they kept raising the price and scaring off potential buyers. Rita had wanted to sell quick, and she didn't mind knocking off a big chunk of the price when Odelia and her parents had expressed an interest.

"Hey, honey," said Rita now. "How have you been? And how are your folks?"

"Great," said Odelia as she stepped inside. "Mom and Dad, too," she added as she removed her shoes at Rita's instigation and accepted the slippers she handed her.

"I'm sorry about that," said Rita. "I run a clean house, so I keep annoying people by making them take off their shoes."

"Oh, no, it's fine," said Odelia. "I walk around in slippers at home, too. It's a lot easier to clean, isn't it?"

"It's because I have so many carpets," Rita said, indicating a nice Persian rug in her living room. "And hardwood floors. If it were tile, like I had in Harrington Street, I wouldn't mind so much. Tile is so easy to clean. These floors and carpets, though."

The house looked squeaky clean, Odelia had to admit. In fact it looked a lot cleaner than her own place, but then she was a busy bee, and so was Chase, and with four cats it was hard to keep up. Or at least that was her excuse and she was sticking to it.

"So what can I do for you?" asked Rita as she took a seat

in the living room salon, where several couches were lined up around a big-screen television. Flowers were everywhere, and plants, and it was obvious Rita missed having her own backyard. She'd been an avid gardener back in the day, and had intimated it was the only thing about having a house that she would miss when she moved into the apartment.

"This is a little delicate, Rita," said Odelia. "And maybe you shouldn't hear this from me, but…"

Rita frowned. "What's wrong? Did something happen?"

"My mom has issues with her plumbing," said Odelia, deciding to take this from the top.

"Oh, well, I'm not sure I can help you with that. Back when we lived there, there were always issues with the plumbing. Old house, you know. What can you do?"

"I know. So she had Gwayn Partington come over, and he knocked out a piece of wall in the basement, looking for the connection to the water main."

"Okay," said Rita, not flinching or indicating she knew where this was going.

Odelia took a deep breath and plunged in. "He found a skeleton stuck in the wall. A skeleton that must have been there for several decades."

Rita's eyes went wide and she brought a hand to her face. "Oh, no," she said.

"I think it's your father, Rita. In fact, I'm almost positive that it is."

"Dad," said Rita in a hoarse whisper. "Oh, God."

"Yeah. So I expect my uncle to pay you a visit as soon as they've made a positive ID, but I figured I owe it to you to give the news personally, as we have a connection and I…"

Rita nodded, speechless, her eyes brimming with tears. "Thanks," she said.

"Do you have any idea how he could have ended up down there?" she asked.

Rita was shaking her head, still making valiant efforts to control herself. "No," she said finally. "I mean, someone must have put him there, right? If it's really him, someone must have..." She blinked and reached for the box of Kleenex on the coffee table. "I never thought he ran away, like Mom thought. He was too loving a father to do that to us."

"Your mom thought he ran away?"

"She did. He'd gotten into some trouble at work. I don't remember the details. Also there was talk about a fight he had with a work friend over a loan or something. So the police at the time thought he'd run away when he realized he couldn't repay the loan. Dad worked with some unsavory characters, and some of those fellas wouldn't have taken kindly to not being repaid when someone borrowed money from them, so..."

"But you never believed that."

"No, I didn't. Dad loved me—loved us. We were a very warm, loving family, and he wouldn't simply leave us. Just... vanish without a trace and not give us a sign of life for all those years. Mom died not knowing what had happened to him, you know, and until the very end she wondered—we all did, actually. Me, Mom and my brother."

"Tom. Does he still live around here?"

"Brooklyn. He's a Wall Street guy. He's retired now, though. In fact he's thinking about giving up his apartment and permanently moving back to Hampton Cove. One of the downstairs flats is up for sale, and he's seriously considering putting down an offer." She wiped at her eyes. "Oh, Odelia. Whatever I expected when I saw your face on the intercom just now, it definitely wasn't this."

"I'm sorry to be the bearer of such bad news," said Odelia ruefully.

"It's not bad news," said Rita with a brave smile. "It's good news. Now I know Dad never left us. Now I know what really happened, and how he was with us all this time."

"Yeah, he was right there," said Odelia softly.

"Amazing," said Rita as she gave this some more thought. "How he was right beneath our feet all these years, and we didn't know." She directed a resolute look at Odelia. "You're a private detective, aren't you?"

"Um, not really. I'm a reporter for the *Hampton Cove Gazette*."

"But you do some private detecting on the side, right?"

"I don't have a license, so it's not official," she said. "I help out my uncle and my boyfriend from time to time. Civilian consultant, they call it." She had a feeling Rita was working towards something, and she had a pretty good idea what it could be.

"Can you find out what happened to my dad? Please? For my sake and Tom's? Someone must have put him inside that wall, right? He didn't crawl in there all by himself and brick himself in, did he?"

"No, I don't think he did," said Odelia, treading carefully now. "It seems very unlikely that he would have done such a thing."

"Exactly. So he was *murdered*. Someone *killed* him and had the gall—the impudence—to bury him in his own house, right under our noses—underneath the feet of his wife and family. Please find out who did it, Odelia. I don't have a lot of money, but I'll talk to Tom. He has some money saved up, and I'm sure he'll agree with me to hire you."

"No, please, Rita," said Odelia, holding up her hand. "I'm not going to accept any money from you. I'll look into your father's death, not for money, but because I want to know, too. You see, people in this town like to gossip, and already they're talking about my grandmother being the one who put that body there. So it's important for me to find out what really happened, and to prove Gran innocent."

"Your gran! How could she possibly be involved?"

"Oh, you know what people are like. Gran went through an acrimonious divorce back in the day, and then my grandfather died, so now they think she killed him and—"

"Buried him in the basement? That's ludicrous. Your grandmother didn't even live there back then. We lived there, and continued living there for many years afterward."

"Exactly, which is why…" She swallowed. "Can I show you something?"

"Of course. I'm sorry for being so emotional," said Rita, who seemed more composed now. "It's been a long time, and I always thought I was over my dad's disappearance, but this was a big surprise, and it's going to be a big surprise for my brother, too."

Odelia took out her phone and showed Rita a picture of the skeleton she'd taken.

The woman sat stony-faced for a moment, then burst out, "Oh, my poor daddy."

"I'm sorry," said Odelia, then flicked through to the picture of the brooch she'd taken. "Do you have any idea what this could be? It was found at the same spot."

Rita took Odelia's phone, and pinched the picture out with her fingers, making it bigger. "It looks like a brooch of some kind," she said.

"It is. It looks very valuable. Diamonds, probably."

Rita shook her head. "I've never seen it before. Definitely not ours. Dad was a gardener, and Mom was a stay-at-home mom until after he disappeared. We weren't rich. And definitely not diamond-brooch rich."

"So you have no idea how it could have ended up buried along with your father?"

"No idea," said Rita, and Odelia could see that the woman

wasn't lying. She had absolutely no idea what that brooch was, or where it had come from.

Odelia put her phone away. "Thank you so much, Rita. Now, to get me launched on the investigation, tell me everything you can remember about your father's final days, weeks, or even months. Anything you think might shed light on his disappearance."

"On his murder," said Rita quietly. "Yes, of course. Anything you need. Anything at all."

CHAPTER 15

"You see, we were a loving and a warm family, as I've already said, but of course, like in any family, there were tensions," Rita said as she got up. "Do you want some tea? I don't know if you remember this, but I'm an expert on weird herbal concoctions."

"Yes, thank you," said Odelia, who did remember. And as Rita disappeared into the kitchen, she threw her mind back to the time Rita Baker had been her neighbor. She distinctly remembered Rita as a cool neighbor, who never failed to say hi, or to babysit when Mom and Dad went out on the weekends. Rita had quickly become a friend of the family, and Odelia had been in and out of her house often, spending many a night on the couch watching TV together. She remembered her as warm-hearted and fun. Happy to babysit because she didn't have kids herself, even though she always wanted them. She never married, though, and the family she'd hoped to have never materialized. She had boyfriends, though, which Odelia would see sitting out on the deck having breakfast in the morning. Whenever Rita babysat she would never have a boyfriend over, though. She was strict that way, which is why Marge and Tex entrusted her with their kid so much.

"So I have the usual, rosehip and linden and chamomile," said Rita, offering her a selection of teas. "And then I have my special blends," she added with a smile, and spirited a second box into her hands. "This is the stuff I keep for special occasions."

"Oh, no, I couldn't," said Odelia.

"Nonsense. We're old friends, you and I, and if I can't share my special blend with you, who can I share it with? Besides, Tom, bless his heart, hates tea with a vengeance. Devil's brew, he calls it. He only drinks coffee, and especially all of that horrible Starbucks stuff. I'm afraid Wall Street has seduced him to the dark side." She laughed.

"Does he have kids?" asked Odelia, vaguely remembering Tom.

"No kids. Staunch bachelor, that one. And I don't think he'll change now. My little brother is seventy-one, if you can believe it. I can hardly believe it myself. Or the fact that I'm seventy-six now."

Odelia smiled, and selected one of the oriental blends she hoped she'd like.

"Excellent choice, young lady," said Rita primly, and disappeared into the kitchen again. Soon Odelia could hear the kettle boiling, and Rita called out "So how is your grandmother?"

"She's fine. Acting a little weird from time to time, but nothing we can't handle."

"You mean she hasn't changed? Why doesn't that surprise me? Do you remember she used to read you ghost stories? And when you couldn't sleep afterward you had to go and sleep with your mom and dad because you were afraid of all the monsters?"

Odelia laughed. She hadn't remembered but did now.

"Gran always loved stirring up trouble," she said as Rita returned, carrying a teapot and cups and saucers on a platter.

She placed them on the coffee table along with a box of cookies. "So as I said, my mom and dad fought from time to time, but never anything too serious. The usual stuff, you know. I do remember they used to fight about my dad associating with the wrong crowd, as my mother called it. Those unsavory work friends I mentioned."

Odelia picked out a cookie and took a sip from her tea. She closed her eyes. "This stuff is amazing."

"Delish, right? I love it. Got it from a little tea shop in Manhattan that my brother once showed me. He knows I like my teas."

"You and your brother are pretty close, huh?"

"Oh, yes, we are. I guess it's the curse of being left without a dad. Either you drift apart as a family, or you stick together. We stuck together like glue after Dad disappeared. Became thick as thieves, the three of us, and now, after Mom passed, the two of us."

"When did your mom pass?"

"Um, ten years ago? She was ninety-four, and doing great right up until the end. She was in a nursing home. Well, you would know. She moved there when your mom and dad bought the house."

"She was there for a long time, then?"

"Yeah, fifteen years. She never thought she'd last that long, but she had a great spirit and was blessed with excellent health. So we were lucky we had her for so long, my brother and I." She smiled as she remembered her mother with obvious affection.

"So... these unsavory people your dad associated with, do you think they could have had something to do with his death?"

"I have no idea. I just know it's the first thing that comes to mind. Of course, they'll all be gone now, so it will be hard to find out anything about them. I just remember he was away a lot at some point, and usually with the same crew of people. And Mom always forbade them the house, arguing she didn't want their bad influence to rub off on us."

"Do you remember any names? Places they used to hang out? Anything like that?"

Rita nodded slowly as she thought back. "Um... They used to have a place where they met after work, shooting pool and hanging out. The Rusty Beaver, I think it was called. It's not there anymore, though. It's a flower shop these days, of all things. And the names..." She shook her head. "I'd have to ask my brother. He's aces with names."

"Well, please ask him and I'll see if I can find out some more about these people."

"Do you think the police will look into my dad's murder?"

"I'm sure they will. Even though it's a cold case, they'll want to know what happened."

"It's going to be hard, though, right? It's been..." She closed her eyes, then nodded. "Fifty-five years. Hard to imagine it's been so long. I was twenty-one when he disappeared, still living at home, and Tom was sixteen. My mom used to burn a candle for dad each year on the anniversary of his disappearance, telling us it might bring him back. A light to guide him home." She smiled as tears trickled down her cheeks again. "I'm sorry."

"No, don't apologize. I can't imagine how I would feel if my dad suddenly walked out and never came back. And fifty-five years later I discover he was actually murdered."

"Yeah, it's tough, not knowing. That's the hardest part. I sometimes think it would have been easier if we'd have found him immediately, but of course now I'll never know."

"So... your brother will get back to me about the names thing?" said Odelia, feeling slightly embarrassed to keep asking her reporter questions while the woman was in obvious distress.

But Rita pulled herself together, wiped away her tears and nodded. "I'll call him now. I want to be the one to tell him about what happened."

Odelia nodded. She'd taken out her notebook. "Your dad used to work for Courtyard Living, a landscaping company. Any idea if they're still in business?"

"They might be."

"I'll have a dig. They might have an archive. Old personnel files."

"Might be worth pursuing," Rita agreed.

"Anything else that might be important?"

"Can't think of anything right now, but if something occurs to me that I think might shed some light on his disappearance—his murder—I'll call you, okay?"

"Please do," said Odelia. "And please call me even if you don't have anything to share and just want to talk."

"I'll do that," Rita said with a warm smile. "God, how long has it been? Five years? It seems like yesterday that you were that adorable little girl with pigtails sitting on my lap."

"You were the best babysitter I ever had, Rita. I mean that."

"Yeah, I loved our evenings together, pigging out in front of the TV, watching until we both fell asleep."

Odelia laughed. "Even watching stuff I wasn't supposed to be watching."

"Hey, what are cool babysitters for, huh?"

"Thanks, Rita," she said fondly.

"Why didn't we stay in touch?"

"I guess life got in the way,"

"Yeah, I guess it did. Well, let's keep in touch now. You may be too old to need a babysitter, but you're never too old to need a friend. And who knows, one day you may have kids yourself, and need the best babysitter in the world to keep an eye on them."

"If that happens, you'll be the first person I call," she promised, getting up.

Both women hugged, and then Rita walked her to the door. And as she opened it, the doorbell chimed merrily though the hallway and Rita frowned. "Now who could that be?" And as they both watched, Odelia wasn't surprised to see her uncle and Chase.

She grinned. "And that, my dear, sweet Rita, is my boyfriend Chase Kingsley."

CHAPTER 16

*H*is last patient had left, and so Tex was leaning back in his chair and stretching his arms behind his head. He loved his job, but at the end of a long day at the office he was glad to go home and relax. He was lucky that he had a wonderful family. A wife he adored, a daughter he loved, a mother-in-law… who wasn't always as horrible as she could be.

He got up, grabbed his coat from the rack and opened the door a crack. Vesta had already left for the day. Unlike most employees she never said hi in the morning, and never said see ya in the evening. She simply showed up and left without announcing either arrival or departure. He'd learned to live with it, though at first it had irked him a little. A garrulous and kindly man himself, he loved chatting with people, and he would have loved a receptionist who dropped in from time to time between patients to shoot the breeze.

In that sense he sometimes regretted setting up his own practice. He wouldn't have minded working at a hospital, or even in a group practice with other doctors. Sometimes he dreamed of meeting his colleagues in the canteen and talking about what was on TV last night around the water cooler or the coffee machine. What he had, instead, was Vesta, who, more often than not, could be grumpy and annoying. And unlike some receptionists of colleagues he sometimes met at conferences or seminars, she didn't even bring him his coffee in the morning, something she strongly felt he should do himself.

He glanced around the office, then walked out, closing the door behind him. He walked home, whistling a happy tune as he did, and remembered the idea that had occurred to him earlier in the day, about launching a singing career. He needed a hobby, so why not singing? He could maybe start small, by doing a couple of shows at local eateries, and gauge the response. If he was good enough he could even audition for *The Voice* or *American Idol* or *America's Got Talent* and get some visibility that way. He didn't want to become a star. All he wanted was to meet some nice people and have some fun.

So when he arrived home and let himself in with his key, the first thing he did was move down into the basement to check out the space he'd chosen to launch his singing career. When he arrived, he saw that someone had knocked out part of the back wall, and remembered how Marge had told him about the plumbing issues. He hoped the problem had been fixed. He glanced around and imagined building a small stage and installing a state-of-the-art sound system. If only he could convince colleagues like Denby Jennsen in Happy Bays and Cary Horsfield in Hampton Keys to join him, they could even form a band. The Singing Doctors. It would just be about the fun and the camaraderie, of course. And as he stood there, dreaming of a roseate future in which all four coaches of *The Voice* turned their chairs for The Singing Doctors, suddenly Vesta walked in from the next part of the basement, and growled, "Out of my way, landlubber."

She was carrying boxes of rice and dumped them on the floor in the corner.

"Hey, Vesta," he said. "So what's cooking?"

She merely directed a curious eye at the ceiling. "What do you think? If we reinforced this ceiling, do you think it could withstand a nuclear blast?"

His eyes traveled up to the ceiling, which was plastered but not exactly nuclear-blast-proofed. "Um… why?" he asked, though it was probably a stupid question.

"To survive the nuclear winter, numbnuts. What do you think? Now I figure if we're going to survive in here, you, me and Marge, we gotta dig deeper. Create more space."

"Dig d… deeper?" he asked, staring at his mother-in-law the way he'd been staring at her for what seemed like his entire life.

"Sure. And if you want to add Odelia and Chase, we'll probably need to go even deeper. Though I figure screw 'em. They can dig their own bunker next door. What do you reckon?"

"Bunker? Next door?"

"Oh, don't just stand there like a chump. Give me a hand with the potatoes."

And she dumped a bag of potatoes into his arms.

He now saw she'd probably bought up the store's entire stock of spuds.

"So is this for a party?" he asked. "Are you organizing a surprise party?"

"Haven't you been listening? I'm building a bunker. To survive the nuclear winter, though it could also be a flood, at the rate the oceans are rising, or a tsunami, or a tornado. Take your pick. Or volcanoes. If Yellowstone explodes, you know we're all screwed, right? So better get cracking, bud, and count your lucky stars we have a house to call our own. Think about the poor bastards who live in an apartment.

They'll be wiped out first. So where do you think we should start drilling?"

*W*hen Marge arrived home ten minutes later, it was a pale and visibly distraught Tex who emerged from the basement. The first thing she thought was that the skeleton was still down there, and she now remembered she'd totally forgotten to tell him about that. But when her husband uttered the word Vesta, she knew it wasn't the skeleton that had scared the living daylights out of him, but her mother. Now why wasn't she surprised?

CHAPTER 17

"*B*rutus, you have to get me out of here," Harriet said, not for the first time.

"I know, sugar muffin, but I can't. Your head seems to be really, really stuck in there."

"Damn mouse," Harriet grumbled. "If I get my paws on that horrible creature, I'll tear her limb from limb and then stomp on her remains. Ouch!" she yelled when Brutus had grabbed hold of her butt and tried pulling her in a straight line away from the wall.

"I'm sorry," he said. "I think we need a helping paw here."

"No way. Uh-uh. I'm not going to suffer the indignation of anyone finding out about this," she said decidedly. "No one can know this happened, Brutus. Promise me."

"Okay," he said without conviction. "I just don't think we'll be able to get you out of this wall all by ourselves. We're going to need tools and we're going to need Odelia."

"Brutus, read my lips. No one can know."

It was hard to read her lips, as they were stuck along with her head inside the wall, but Brutus could see where she was coming from all the same.

"Look," she said, "can't you just… pick away at the wall until you've dug a hole big enough to get my head out?"

"Trust me, I've been picking away like nobody's business, but the only thing that's worn down by now is my claws. This old wall is a lot tougher than it looks."

"I'm hungry, Brutus, and I'm getting a cramp. Literally a pain in the neck."

"I know, sweet peach. Just hang in there. At some point someone will come and they'll get you out of your horrible predicament in a snap."

She was silent for a moment. She hated to be exposed to ridicule. If there was one thing she feared more than anything else in life, it was to be the object of mirth, to be laughed at, to be the laughingstock of the town's cat population. And laugh they would.

"I could get Max and Dooley," said Brutus. "If you tell them not to tell anyone, they'll do it, right?"

"I wouldn't be too sure," she said softly.

"But they're our friends. And Dooley adores you."

"I know he does. And it's not his loyalty that worries me. It's the fact that he's not smart enough to keep his big trap shut. He can't help it. He'll promise me not to tell a soul, and the next moment we'll be down in the park for cat choir and he'll be shooting his mouth off. Not because he means bad, but just because that's how he is."

"What about Max? Do you think he'll blab?"

"Oh, no, he won't. Max is true to his word, and smart enough not to talk."

"We could always tell Dooley a story."

"What story?"

"We could tell him… you've been exploring. That you decided to explore what's behind these walls, and now you need help getting your big discovery out of there."

"Could work," she admitted. "Dooley is probably dumb enough to believe it, too."

"I don't think Dooley is necessarily dumb," said Brutus. "I just think he's... naive."

"Well, whatever he is, he can't be allowed to blab about this. He just can't."

Brutus nodded, even though Harriet wasn't in a position to see it. "You know, I'm the latest addition to the team, right?"

"Uh-huh," she said.

"But I want to tell you how much I've come to appreciate you, and Max and Dooley, too," he said, suddenly feeling maudlin. He glanced around the basement, which looked dark and dank and, with Harriet being stuck in the wall, a little scary, too.

"I know, Brutus. And I also know that you and Max didn't get along at first, but that you've become fast friends, and I can't even begin to tell you how happy that makes me."

"It does?" he asked, smiling. "That's great."

"Yes, and I also understand you're suddenly feeling talkative and philosophical and ruminating on life and all of that, but right now I need you to focus, all right, wookie? And I need you to get me out of here, for even though we can try to tell Dooley that I'm an urban explorer, I'm not sure the story will stick, so if you can get me out of here before anyone shows up, that would make me love you even more than I already do."

"Okay, great," he said, getting up. "I'll give it another shot."

And as he took a firm hold on her shoulders and pulled, while she wriggled to try and get her head dislodged, in a corner of the basement sat an entire family of mice watching the scene and snickering freely. They consisted of Molly and Rupert and nearly all of their four-hundred-strong offspring. Molly had felt this was a sight they'd never seen before and she was right. It rarely happened, at least outside Tom and Jerry cartoons, that a cat was bested by a mouse, and she felt this had an educational value that was hard to overstate. And as they all chuckled and snickered at Brutus's attempts to free his lady love, all Molly could think was that she would give a million bucks if she had a phone right now and could film the whole thing and throw it up on YouTube.

She was pretty sure it would set the cause of cats against mice back about a millennium, or even more, and give mice the world over fresh hope in their eternal battle against their age-old nemesis. It might also deal a significant psychological blow to cats everywhere, and make them think twice about trying to attack mice in their lair.

But mice don't carry smartphones, and it's hard for them to create a YouTube account, so for now she'd have to suffice with her four hundred kids prodding each other in the midriff and rolling on the floor laughing and generally having a grand old time.

CHAPTER 18

$\mathcal{T}$he lights in the kitchen had been turned on, and from the noise inside and the sound of voices it was clear that our humans had finally returned home from work.

So Dooley and I jumped down from the swing and stood in front of the kitchen door and applied our front paws to it, scratching until someone inside heard us and decided to open the door. When finally they did and Marge appeared, Dooley said, "I could have gone in through the pet flap and told Marge to open the door, couldn't I, Max?"

"That's right, you could have," I agreed. And it just goes to show how famished we both were that a simple idea like that hadn't even occurred to either of us.

We both moved in the direction of our bowls and moments later we were tucking in. You may wonder why cats need a double set of bowls, over there in Marge's house and at Odelia's, but then my answer would be, of course we need double bowls. The same way humans like to go out to restaurants or the diner or a snack bar or order Chinese, we like to source our food from as many places as felinely possible. And can you blame us?

"Could you tell Odelia to open the sliding glass door, Marge?" I asked.

"Oh, honey, I don't know when she'll be home. She's on a case, and you know what she's like. She might be gone all night. Can't you go through the pet flap?"

"No," I said, though I wasn't prepared to elaborate.

"Max doesn't fit through the pet flap," said Dooley, who doesn't mind elaborating on my behalf, even though I hadn't even signed him a power of attorney or anything.

"You can't fit through the pet flap?" asked Marge with a frown. "Let's see. Try to go through now, Max. Yes, just give it a go… Oh, dear."

Following her instructions, I'd gotten stuck again, of course, much to my embarrassment. Marge made short shrift of my predicament by shoving me through, and then she opened the door for me again so I could return indoors.

She studied me for a moment with a critical eye. "Did Odelia put you on that diet she mentioned?"

"Um…" I said, stalling for time.

"She forgot," said Dooley. "After Vena told us about the diet you guys all went vegetarian, and then you all turned carnivore again, and the diet thing fell off the radar."

Marge smiled. "Good summary, Dooley. I see the whole picture now."

"Thanks, Marge," said Dooley, pleased as punch.

"And about that diet, I think you need to go on it again, Max. If you don't even fit through the pet door…"

"Isn't it possible that the pet flap shrank?" I said. "Heat expands wood, but cold makes it contract, right? So isn't it possible that even though I lost weight that the pet door simply shrank in size?"

"I doubt it," said Marge. "The pet flap is made of plastic,

and plastic doesn't expand or contract as much as wood does. No, I'm afraid there's only one solution for you, Max. Lose weight, or otherwise spend your nights outside, and return inside in the morning."

I shivered at the quaint notion. "Spend my nights outside? But the nights are getting colder, Marge. And you know what I think about the cold. I don't like it."

"So slim down a little, and fit right through that door again." She crouched down next to me. "See, Max, that pet flap is your weight control tool. As long as you fit through there, your weight is fine. When you don't fit anymore, it's time to slim down. See how easy it is? Fit? Fine. Don't fit? Time to go on a diet."

"Uh-huh," I said, not fully convinced. "I still think the trouble is the door, not me."

"Well, then you won't mind sleeping outside from now on," she said, getting up.

Humans. Not an ounce of compassion with a pet-flap-challenged cat.

"So what happened to Harriet and Brutus?" asked Marge as she picked up a bucket of water and placed it on the drain board.

"Next door, probably," I said as I watched her wash her hands.

It's a habit that frankly annoys me: each time my humans touch me, they wash their hands. Now why is that, I wonder? Am I as dirty as all that? I don't think so. In fact I think my grooming capacity is far superior to any human's. And still *they* wash *their* hands after they touch *me*. Weird, right? And so I immediately started grooming myself. After all, she had touched me, with those dirty pre-washed hands. And as I sat there, carefully removing every hint of human scent from my precious fur, Gran stalked in. "Can you please tell that husband of yours to remove his head from his ass?" she asked.

"Oh, help," said Dooley, wide-eyed. "We need a doctor!"

"Tex is a doctor, Dooley," I reminded him.

"But Tex has his head stuck! He needs a second doctor to remove it!"

I craned my neck to see this medical miracle. How does a human manage to get their head stuck in such an awkward position? But when Tex walked in he looked fine. His head was a little red, but not stuck anywhere, and definitely not up his own bottom.

"It's a miracle!" Dooley cried. "A medical miracle!"

"What is it now?" asked Marge, not all that excited about this miracle.

"*Your* husband objects to *my* plans to keep this family safe from harm!" Gran said.

"Of course I do!" Tex cried, his head reddening even more. "Has she told you about her crazy plan?"

"What plan?" asked Marge in an even tone. She had poured water from the bucket into a small basin and was now rinsing tomatoes and a head of lettuce.

"She wants to turn our basement into a bunker. A nuclear bunker!"

"Not a nuclear bunker, you mug. A regular old bunker that can withstand anything. A nuclear blast, tsunami, hurricane or even Yellowstone going and blowing up on us."

"And why do we need a bunker like that?" asked Marge in the same dispassionate tone as she took a pot roast out of the fridge and sniffed at it.

"Because winter is coming, if you hadn't heard, and we need to protect ourselves."

"Winter is coming but we don't need no nuclear bunker to ride it out," said Tex.

"The *nuclear* winter is coming," Gran specified. "And we

do need a bunker to protect us from the blast. Why do you think Mark Zuckerberg is buying up half of New Zealand? Or those other tech billionaires? These guys know stuff we don't, and they're ready. So do you really want to be the chump that has to watch how his family is blown away by a nuclear explosion because he was too stubborn to listen to his whip-smart ma-in-law?"

"Where do you *get* all this nonsense?" Tex demanded.

"The YouTube, where else? Because the YouTube knows. The YouTube never lies."

"Oh, God," said Tex, and reached for the fridge.

"What are you doing?" asked Marge.

"I need a yogurt."

"Not before dinner, you don't. You know sugar spoils your appetite."

"Your mother spoils my appetite."

"The nuclear winter will spoil your appetite. In fact it will spoil your life. In that it will an-ni-hi-late you!" said Gran, wagging a bony finger in her son-in-law's face.

I glanced to Dooley, and he glanced at me, and then we moved, as one cat, in the direction of the door. A couple of plaintive meows later and Marge was dutifully opening the door again and we were both walking out of the house. Even though winter was coming and it was chilly out, and pouring rain, it was still preferable to being inside.

Usually I don't mind some light entertainment from the Gran-and-Tex show, but I'd had a rough day, what with finding out I needed to diet again, and getting stuck in the pet flap a couple of times, so my tolerance levels were low and about to hit rock bottom.

We walked through the hole in the hedge and into the next garden and then up to the house. No lights were on inside, so Odelia hadn't arrived home yet. I gave the pet flap a sad glance and hunkered down on the deck, while Dooley ventured inside to see if he couldn't wrangle up a human to act as my butler. Meanwhile, I took a well-deserved nap. What? Do you think cats would be as gracious and strong and flexible and overall fantastic if we didn't get our eighteen hours of sleep? Sleep is good for you, you should probably try it sometime, young Padawan. And then I nodded off. Odd, though, but the last sounds that reached my ears were the sounds of Harriet and Brutus shouting.

CHAPTER 19

"*W*hat are you doing here?" asked Chase when Odelia walked out of the building just as he and Uncle Alec were walking in.

"Oh, this and that," said Odelia. "Working on a new piece for the *Gazette*."

Uncle Alec narrowed his eyes at her. "You're investigating the skeleton case, aren't you?"

"And what if I am? If I had to wait for you guys to share information I could have waited a long time."

"Alec thought it best not to involve you," said Chase, happily throwing his boss under the bus.

"That's not what I said, Chase. What I said was that since Odelia is so closely connected to the case, the body being found in her mother's basement, we probably should keep her out of it."

"It's okay," said Odelia. "Maybe by working separately we'll discover a lot more."

"But I don't want you to work separately," said Uncle Alec, looking pained. "I want you not involved in this case at all, you understand?"

"I do understand," she said. "But you have to understand that when my editor gives me an assignment it's a little hard for me to turn him down. Him being my boss and signing my paychecks and all." She gave her uncle a smile which he didn't reciprocate.

"So that's how you want to play this, mh?" he finally asked.

"It seems I don't have a choice, as you decided for me what role I should play."

"I should have known you'd get involved somehow," said her uncle, raking his meaty paw across the few remaining strands of thinning hair on top of his scalp.

"See?" said Chase. "I told you."

"No, you didn't," Alec grumbled. "Well, fine. What did you find out?"

She feigned ignorance. "Find out? What do you mean?"

"Look, if we're going to do this, we better join forces."

"But that's just it. You don't want to join forces."

He raised his eyes heavenward and emitted a rumbling groan. It had started raining, and his groan competed nicely with the sounds of thunder shaking the earth.

"Fine," he finally said. "Have it your way."

"Fine," she said. "I'll crack this case while you run around in circles."

Chase grinned. He was effectively caught in the middle of this inter-family competition. He didn't seem overly troubled, though.

Alec waved a finger in his deputy's face. "If you so much as breathe a single word about this investigation to my niece, you're off this case, Kingsley. Is that clear?"

"Crystal, sir," said Chase.

"Are you people coming up?" suddenly a voice shouted down from the second floor. Rita was leaning out the window and giving them a wave.

"We better go in," Alec muttered and stomped through the door and into the hallway.

Chase gave Odelia a quick peck on the lips. "See you later, babe. Don't wait up for me. When he's in this mood it could take a while."

"So did the skeleton belong to Boyd Baker?"

"Uh-huh," said Chase. "Dental records confirmed it."

"And the brooch?"

"Still haven't been able to figure out who it belonged to."

"Are you coming or what?!" Uncle Alec shouted from inside, holding the door.

"I better not keep the big guy waiting," said Chase. "He might pop a vessel."

❧

I'd been lounging out on that deck for what felt like an eternity when Dooley finally returned from his expedition.

"And?" I said, though I could see from the look on his face that his mission had been for naught.

"No, Odelia isn't home," he said, confirming my suspicions. "And neither is Chase. In fact there isn't any human activity in the house."

"No human activity? You mean there is…"

"Yes, there is feline activity, though I'm not sure what it's all about. I thought I heard voices so I went in search of their source and discovered they came from the basement. But when I put my ear against the door I heard Harriet shouting, 'Push harder. Harder!' 'I'm pushing as hard as I can!' Brutus replied. 'Now pull! Pull as hard as you can! Harder!' 'I'm pulling as hard as I can,' Brutus responded. And then Harriet said 'Push! Push as hard as you can. Yes, yes, that's it! That's it! Oh, that's the spot, Brutus!'"

I cleared my throat. It was obvious to me what was going on here. Brutus and Harriet had decided to take advantage of this lull in the proceedings—a house devoid of humans and pets—to take their relationship to the next level. Though why they'd chosen an inhabitable place like the basement was momentarily beyond me. But then I saw what must have happened. They'd gone down there to chase away those mice, and having done that must have decided to stick around, Harriet falling for Brutus's fatal attraction, and Brutus falling for hers, and the rest, as they say, was history.

"What do you think they're doing, Max?" asked Dooley, looking worried.

I cleared my throat again. It was imperative to protect Dooley's innocence in these times, when unbridled sensuality seems to be all the rage. "Oh, nothing special," I said.

"Is that what they call hanky panky?" asked Dooley, and I stared at him.

"How do you know about hanky panky?"

"Someone from cat choir told me last week. Brutus and Harriet were in the bushes during a break and when I asked Missy what they were doing, she said they were doing hanky panky. But when I asked what hanky panky was, she refused to explain it to me, and said I had to ask someone else."

"So did you?" I asked nervously. "Ask somebody else?"

"Well, I asked Shanille, and she said it is a form of entertainment grownups like to engage in. She was a little fuzzy on the details, though. So then I asked Milo, because Milo always knows his stuff, and he said hanky panky is when two people, or two cats like in this case, are in love and pull each other's tails. So Brutus pulls Harriet's tail and then Harriet pulls Brutus's tail. He said it's a game they like to play and they derive a lot of pleasure from it. But when I asked Misty to pull my tail she slapped me. So then I told her all I wanted to do was some hanky panky with her and she slapped me again."

"You can't just walk up to a cat and ask to do hanky panky with them, Dooley."

"No, I guess I learned that the hard way."

"It's like Milo said, you have to be in love."

"So is that what Brutus and Harriet are doing down there?"

"Yes. Yes, that's exactly what they're doing," I said. "Brutus and Harriet love hanky panky, and I think we better leave them to it and make sure we don't disturb them when they're in the middle of… pulling each other's tails."

"That's what I thought. And that's why I didn't even bother knocking or asking if they were all right down there."

"You did the right thing, Dooley. Never disturb two cats when they're in the middle of hanky panky. Simply stay away and leave them to it."

"Do you think they managed to chase those mice away, though?"

"Well, if they're having fun they must have gotten the job done. Responsible adults always finish the job first, and then engage in some light entertainment."

Dooley smiled. "Good. I wouldn't have slept tonight knowing there were all these mice traipsing all over the house. Not that I have something against mice, but this is our house, Max, and mice have no business here."

"Exactly right, Dooley," I agreed. "It's our house and anyone who dares to enter is what we call an intruder. So when you see a mouse—even though I'm sure Brutus and Harriet managed to convince them to move out—simply yell stranger danger as loud as you can. Then me, Odelia or Chase will come running and we'll chase the intruder away."

He smiled a happy smile and we both lay down and stared out at the rain lashing the backyard. The grass was completely wet, with puddles forming everywhere, and the sky was a nice pitch black. The only lights we could see were those of the neighboring houses, and I could even see smoke wafting from the chimney of the house next door.

Somehow it gave me a cozy feeling, though it would have been even better if we'd been inside, nice and warm and dry, looking out through the window. Then again, beggars can't be choosers, and cats with a little extra volume around the midsection can't hope to fit through the pet flap without losing a couple of pounds.

"Do you think you'll ever fit through that pet flap again, Max?" asked Dooley.

"Oh, I'm sure I will. In fact I have devised a plan that doesn't involve dieting."

"You have?"

"From now on I'm going to take more frequent strolls around the block. More exercise will burn those extra calories, and before you know it I'll be as slim as you."

"That sounds like a great plan, Max. So you won't have to diet?"

"Nope. I can keep on eating exactly what I'm eating now, or maybe even a little bit more, and all the activity will burn those calories right off."

"I like it. Only problem is, if I go on these walks with you, won't I become too slim?"

"That's why you need to eat more, buddy. Tuck in and don't stop eating until you feel completely and utterly stuffed. Like a Thanksgiving turkey, right before the slaughter."

Oops. I should probably not have said that.

He gave me a look of confusion. "Slaughter? What do you mean?"

"Um, nothing. Forget I said that."

"Do they slaughter those nice turkeys?"

"No, they don't," I said after a moment's hesitation. "In fact what they do is bring the old turkeys—the ones that are very old and tired—to Vena and then Vena gives them a pill that makes them go to sleep, and then they simply never wake up."

"That's what I thought," he said, looking slightly disturbed by my slip of the tongue. "And that's what Odelia told me happened, and Marge, and Gran. Those poor turkeys are very, very old and so they decide to make the ultimate sacrifice by giving us the opportunity to live even as they go to heaven. Isn't that right, Max?"

"That's exactly right."

"Well, I just hope that next time we visit Vena she won't give us one of those pills by accident. I don't think I want to end up on Marge and Tex's Thanksgiving dinner table with a lot of stuffing in my belly and gravy poured all over me, if you know what I mean."

"I know exactly what you mean, Dooley. And I'm here to tell you this will never, ever happen."

❧

*O*delia had returned to her car, wondering about her next step. She needed to talk to the people Boyd Baker used to work for, if the company still existed, and get a feel for the man's personality and habits. She realized this was probably the hardest case she'd ever worked on. A case that dated back fifty-five years. How would she ever figure out what happened to the man? When all the witnesses and the people who were around that time were probably all dead and buried?

She inserted her key into the ignition and moments later the engine of her old but trusty pickup truck coughed to life. And then she was moving through the driving rain back in the direction of the homestead. She wanted to talk to Max and Dooley and find out if they'd discovered something on their travels. She didn't hold out a lot of hope, figuring that animals have an even shorter lifespan than humans, so there wouldn't be any pets around from the time of the murder. Still, Max and Dooley had come through for her before, and they might very well do so now.

And as she parked her car in front of the house, she briefly wondered about the burgundy Toyota parked across the street from her house. She didn't think she'd ever seen it around, then figured one of the neighbors must have bought themselves a new car. She got out and hurried to the front door, holding her purse over her head to protect her from this sudden and unexpected storm, and let herself into the house.

She searched around for her cats. It was only when she'd called out that suddenly Dooley's head poked in through the pet flap and when he saw her let out a happy though slightly plaintive meow.

"Oh, hey, Dooley," she said. "Where is Max? And where are the others?"

"Max is outside. He still doesn't fit through the pet flap. And Harriet and Brutus are in the basement doing hanky panky so I decided not to bother them."

She laughed. Dooley probably didn't even know what hanky panky was.

"Are they, now?" she said, and thought about checking the basement to see what they were up to for herself. But of course she didn't. She was a firm believer in giving her pets their space, and if Harriet and Brutus were indeed doing what Dooley said they were doing, they deserved to be left in peace and enjoy themselves. So she withdrew her hand from the basement door and went in search of Max. She could hardly wait to hear his report on all the things he'd discovered in the case of the mysterious basement skeleton.

🐾

*W*hile Dooley was inside greeting Odelia, and telling her to open the door so I could get in, I smiled before me at Dooley's quaint conceit. It was a little tough sometimes having to tell Dooley all kinds of stories. Like telling a kid that Santa Claus is real, and that the tooth fairy will come and collect their tooth when they're sleeping. Then again, it was also heart-warming that Dooley was still a baby in a lot of ways, and the responsibility of being both friend and surrogate parent was one I took very seriously.

The door behind me slid open, and I slipped inside. "Finally," I said, immediately moving to the radiator to heat up my chilled bones.

"So what did you find out?" asked Odelia, not wasting time with preliminaries or how-have-you-beens.

"Well, we discovered that there is an animal living in Hampton Cove who's probably the oldest animal alive. According to Kingman she might even be more than fifty years old, or possibly even sixty or seventy, so she was probably alive when the skeleton found its way into that wall."

"Boyd Baker," said Odelia as she put the kettle on for a cup of tea. "That's his name. He used to live next door with his wife and two kids. He died fifty-five years ago, or at least that's when he disappeared from home never to return."

"Boyd Baker," I said, storing up this information. "So we talked to Camilla, who is a macaw, but she refused to cooperate, unfortunately. She seems to have some sort of irrational fear of cats, and kept saying the most insulting things about us."

"She's afraid we'll eat her," said Dooley. "Which made it hard to talk to her."

"Right," said Odelia as she took a cup from the cupboard, selected a tea bag from the tin, and aimed it into the cup. "In other words, you struck out."

"Yes, we did," I admitted.

"Kingman said there might be animals even older than Camilla," said Dooley," but since they're mollusks they probably won't have a lot of interesting things to tell us about this Boyd Baker."

"No, you're absolutely right," said Odelia with a sigh as she took a seat on one of the high kitchen stools, took her notebook from her purse, and studied her notes. Odelia is a very avid note keeper, which is probably a good thing for a reporter. Cats, on the other hand, have to carry all of our notes inside our heads, as we don't have pockets to put a notebook, or the opposable thumbs to handle a pencil. Luckily we have a lot of brain capacity, so we simply file all the information away up there in our noggin for later use.

"We could always go back and visit Camilla again," I suggested. "Maybe this time she'll be more amenable."

"Yes, maybe she was in a bad mood," Dooley agreed.

"If you think it's worth a shot, why not?" said Odelia, and enjoyed her tea for a couple of minutes while she read through her notes.

I wondered where Chase was, but decided not to ask. When Odelia is busy working on a case, or a story, it's best to simply leave her be. Humans function a lot better when they're not interrupted every five seconds.

Which is why the interruption, when it suddenly came, was so annoying.

CHAPTER 20

*M*arge was in the basement, while Gwayn was whacking away at some pipe or other. She winced at the clanging sound and hoped the man knew what he was doing and not destroying what was left of the house's plumbing system.

"There," he finally grunted as he gave the pipe one more whack, possibly as a parting gift. "That should do it."

"So… it's fixed now?" she asked, almost afraid to utter the words in case she might jinx the repairman's magic.

"I hope so." He moved to a corner of the basement and opened the small tap that had been installed there. And when the cool, clear stream spouted from the tap, Marge almost whimpered with delight.

Instead, she clamped her hands together and said, "Oh, thank you so much, Gwayn. I thought I'd never see the day."

"Just a minor issue with a rusted valve," he said as he wiped his hands on a rag then started placing the instruments of his trade back inside his toolbox. "So how about that body? They ever find out who it belonged to?" he asked as he directed a curious gaze at the hole that was still plainly visible in the outer wall.

"My brother says it's Boyd Baker, the man who lived here before we bought the house. My daughter is looking into it, and Alec, of course," she added, wondering why she would put more faith in her daughter's investigative qualities than her brother's. "Tex and I bought the house from Boyd's widow Phyllis. Apparently he disappeared *fifty-five* years ago, and this is where he ended up." She placed extra emphasis on the number fifty-five, just in case Gwayn would be amongst those who thought the body belonged to her dearly departed dad, murdered by her mother.

"The Bakers, huh?" said Gwayn with a frown. "I remember Ma Baker, of course. Didn't she pass away a couple of years ago?"

"Yes, she did. Her daughter and son are still with us, though."

"Yeah, I seem to remember my dad doing some work for the Bakers back in the day. Though I could be wrong, of course. Names and faces," he added apologetically. "My mind is like a sieve. Dad was much better with faces. He could see a person once and never forget what they looked like. Amazing gift, especially in our line of work. Well, then," he said. "I think that should do it. I'll check upstairs and then I'll be off."

"Thank you so much, Gwayn. You're a miracle worker."

"Yeah, well, wouldn't want you to be without water all night, would we?" he said. He moved up the stairs, Marge right behind him. In the kitchen, Vesta and Tex were still arguing about the future of mankind, or Tex's dream of becoming the next winner of *The Voice* and a musical talent to be reckoned with, but when Gwayn walked in they both shut up. They might not like each other very much, but there was one thing they both agreed on: never hang out your dirty laundry for the whole world to see.

Gwayn fiddled with the tap, and when the water ran, Marge heaved a sigh of relief.

"Funny, huh?" said Gwayn, who made no indication to leave, "If it hadn't been for your valve to go bust, I would never have had to take out that piece of wall, and Boyd Baker would never have been found. Weird how things can work out like that. Makes you wonder how many other bodies are buried all over the place, waiting to be found by an enterprising plumber." And with these words he finally took his leave.

"Boyd Baker?" asked Gran. "Is he the dead dude?"

"Yeah, Phyllis Baker's husband, the woman we bought the house from," said Marge.

"Well, I'll be damned," said Gran. "I always thought there was something fishy about that couple."

"Of course you did," said Tex acerbically. "You think there's something fishy about every couple. Or every single person you meet."

"No, I don't. But the Bakers..." She frowned. "I seem to remember hearing stories about Boyd Baker. Stories about how he wasn't as honest as he showed himself to be."

"You mean he was a crook?" asked Marge.

"Yeah, something like that. He was a gardener, right? Used to work for this big landscaping company, and every time he showed up to do a place things would go missing. Jewelry, money, bits and bobs. No one ever accused him of anything, but rumor had it Boyd had a buddy who worked as a fence and could sell whatever Boyd managed to lay his hands on."

"Like that brooch," said Marge. "The brooch they found on him."

"Yeah, but why would whoever killed him leave that

brooch? That doesn't make sense. If he was killed by the person the brooch belonged to, wouldn't they take it?"

"They could have been in a terrible rush."

"Or not thinking straight," said Tex. "Especially if this wasn't a professional hit they may have panicked and forgotten to search his pockets. And in the fifty-five years he was stuck inside that wall, his clothes may have pretty much turned to dust, but that brooch hasn't."

"Food for thought," said Gran, slapping the table and getting up. "Now are we going to eat, or do I have to order Chinese again?"

"I thought you'd be interested in cracking this case," said Marge, surprised by her mother's lack of interest.

"I gave up sleuthing a long time ago," said Gran. "The world is about to end, Marge, so who cares about a couple of stiffs? We'll all be dead soon, unless your husband gets his head out of his ass and turns this basement into a bunker so we can survive. Even then it's gonna be touch and go. I'm not sure any bunker will be able to survive the initial blast, or those three-hundred-foot waves hitting us like sledgehammers, and all of that lava pouring out of those volcanoes, not to mention those volcanic winds. They roll in so hot and fast they'll burn you to a crisp in nanoseconds. So if after the nukes, and the tsunami, and the lava and the volcanic winds this little bunker of ours is still here, and we're still alive, it will be a great, big miracle."

And with these words she got up and started giving her daughter a helping hand.

CHAPTER 21

*'"*e need to act now, Johnny," said Jerry as he watched the lights in the house go out.

"Now? But it's not even eight o'clock."

"Can't you see what's going on? They all moved to the house next door, probably for dinner. We need to hit the place now, while there's nobody there."

"But I thought we were going to wait until after midnight, when they've all gone to bed."

"That was Plan A," said Jerry carefully. Long association with his partner had taught him to always move at the speed of Johnny's intelligence, which was pretty much a snail's pace. If he tried to rush things Johnny could get mulish: he'd refuse to budge until he had the whole thing laid out to him in minute detail. "Look, I asked around, and this broad is the daughter of the people next door, and I'll bet they've all gone over there for dinner, so if we move fast we have the place to ourselves. If we wait until after midnight, we might bump into the cop that lives there. You know how cops suffer from those night terrors, on account of all the trauma and stuff, so he'll probably come traipsing into the kitchen just as we're lifting his nice flatscreen. What?" he asked when he noticed how Johnny sat staring at him with wide eyes. "Why are you looking at me like that?"

"A cop!" said Johnny. "You never said anything about a cop!"

"It doesn't matter! He's next door, enjoying a nice family dinner. The coast is clear, Johnny, but it won't be for long. You know how cops eat. They wolf down their meals and before you know it he'll be flopping down in front of the television to watch ESPN."

"I'm not going in there," said Johnny, shaking his head stubbornly. "You never said anything about a cop and I don't like the idea of burgling a cop's house."

"It's not his house. The place belongs to his girlfriend, some reporter chick."

"Yeah, but if she's dating a cop…"

"Look, I'm going in there and I'm going to take whatever loot I can find. You stay here and act like a pussy. I don't care."

It was a risky move, but one that had worked in the past.

"Okay, fine," said Johnny finally. "I'll go with you. But if we bump into that cop I'll tell him this was your idea."

"Oh, so now you'll rat me out, huh?"

"I didn't know it was a cop's place!"

"It's not a cop's place—oh, rats." He climbed out of the car. Sometimes he wondered if he wouldn't be better off working alone. No endless arguments and no sharing the loot with a partner. But then he figured he'd probably miss the big oaf. Johnny might not have a lot going on up there, but he was basically a happy-go-lucky guy with a sunny personality that complemented Jerry's sour-grapes character extremely well.

Both crooks quickly crossed the road at a trot, checking left and right as they did, and then disappeared into the shadows between the two houses. Emerging at the back, Jerry couldn't believe their good fortune when he found the glass sliding door ajar.

"Un-freakin-believable!" he hissed as he put on his leather gloves and pushed the door further open.

"Yeah, this is a good sign," Johnny agreed, though he still seemed nervous, darting anxious glances to the house next door, where the cop was enjoying his family feast.

They stepped inside and would have made a beeline for the television if Jerry hadn't suddenly noticed a big, fat, red cat lying on the couch and staring at him with its glassy cat's eyes. He shivered. He hated cats. They were even worse than dogs. Next to the fat red creature a smaller gray specimen rested, also watching them intently.

"Hey, kitty, kitty," said Johnny. Though he preferred dogs, he was partial to all creatures great and small.

He reached out a hand to stroke the fat one's fur when Jerry hissed, "Leave those stupid cats alone, will you? This ain't a social call. Grab that TV and put it outside. I'll look upstairs for the jewels and the money."

From experience he knew that most people kept their valuables in the bedroom where they hoped no one would find them. Why this was he didn't know. He would never keep anything in the bedroom, knowing that was where fellow crooks looked first.

He took the stairs two at a time, then moved into the bedroom, lighting his progress with the small penlight he kept just for these occasions. He searched around until he found the dresser and he'd only opened two drawers before he hit the jackpot: a small box filled to the brim with jewels. Earrings, bracelets, pendants, you name it, the reporter chick had it. Most of it wasn't worth much, he could see at first glance, but there were one or two pieces that might fetch them a nice price.

He emptied the box in his shoulder bag and moved to the closet where often a small safe was located. No such luck here. He crossed to the second bedroom, which was some kind of office with an elliptical machine, and searched the drawers. Nothing much, but he took the laptop and the tablet computer. Then he proceeded to room number three and rifled through the closets. He quickly gave up, his expert eyes telling him there was nothing of value stored in there.

He'd arrived back downstairs where Johnny had already done the preliminaries and had searched through all the cupboards and closets and cabinets.

"Any safes?" he asked.

"Nah, nuthing, Jerry."

"Maybe in the basement," he said, and opened the door to the basement. A lot of people kept their safes in the basement, once again because they hoped no one would bother to look there. And as he and Johnny descended the stairs, he saw to his surprise that it was infested with even more cats than upstairs. A black one that looked kinda lost, and a white one that had its head stuck in the wall. "Look at that dumb critter," he said, pointing to the white cat. But Johnny was staring at a part of the wall where someone had recently applied a hammer.

The cats were meowing up a storm, even the one with its head stuck in the wall. They were yowling and howling, making that horrible noise only cats can make, and that will drive you nuts if you listen to it for too long.

"Can't you get them to shut up?" he asked his partner in crime. "If they keep this up someone will come and look."

"Here, kitty, kitty," said Johnny, bending over and trying to attract the attention of the black cat. "Nice kitty, kitty. Sweet little kitty."

But whatever language he was speaking, it clearly made little impression on the cats, for they seemed to increase the volume of their laments.

"Oh, for crying out loud," Jerry grunted. "I can't believe a bunch of stupid cats are going to ruin a perfectly nice burglary."

He'd searched around the basement but had found no evidence of a safe, until he thought he saw something that looked promising: a small cupboard shoved up against the wall. So he opened it and immediately wished he hadn't. Inside the cupboard dozens of mice stared back at him, their beady black eyes eyeing him with distinct malice!

"Yikes!" he shouted. He hated mice even more than he hated cats or dogs.

He jumped back but the mice had apparently not appreciated this intrusion on their privacy and jumped out of the cupboard and attacked!

"Help!" he cried as he tottered back and then stumbled and fell. Immediately he was overrun with mice. They were everywhere: on his head, on his arms, crawling into his shirt and on his bare skin. "Johnny! Help!" he screamed.

"Oh, no, you don't," said Johnny, and took a small cannon from his pocket. And before Jerry could tell him not to, he'd fired his firearm and a minor explosion rocked the basement, tearing a fist-sized hole in the wall. For a moment nothing happened, and then the mice all made a run for it, and raced to the far wall and disappeared.

"Thank God," said Johnny, as he helped up his partner. "Are you all right, Jer?"

"Why did you have to go and fire that gun? And without a frickin' silencer!"

"Well, it worked, didn't it? I scared them off."

"Let's just get out of here," said Jerry, and made for the staircase.

And he'd just put his foot on the first step when suddenly a burly figure appeared on the top step and shouted, "Freeze!"

The figure was also holding a gun in his hand, and looked like he meant business.

CHAPTER 22

"*A* gunfight! In our basement!" Dooley was saying. "First the dead skeleton next door and now a gunfight!"

"Yeah, I feel like I'm in a gangster movie," said Brutus as he licked his paws.

We were all on the couch in the living room while all around us activity buzzed. Cops had shown up en masse, and had taken the two gangsters off Chase's hands, and now they were picking the bullet one of the crooks had fired out of the wall and investigating the loot they'd gathered. Everything lay piled up in a heap on the living room floor, where the gangsters had left it, and amongst the treasure was Odelia's box of jewelry, the television, an envelope with cash Odelia liked to hide in the kitchen drawer for emergencies, and plenty of other stuff. They'd even laid their hands on Chase's laptop, which probably has all kinds of very sensitive information on it about the world of crime and whatnot. And of course the tablet computer we like to use when we need to google something. All in all a nice haul, if they'd gotten away with it.

Unfortunately for them and fortunately for Odelia and Chase we'd quickly slipped out of the house the moment those two thugs had started rummaging through Odelia's private things, and had warned Odelia, and it didn't take long for Chase to come running, armed to the teeth.

"Imagine if they'd gotten away with it," said Harriet now as she stared at the pile of personal possessions.

"Yeah, imagine," said Brutus.

Both Brutus and Harriet appeared a little under the weather, I thought. Then again, an entire afternoon and part of the evening doing hanky panky will wear a cat out.

"So did you enjoy your hanky panky?" asked Dooley now.

Brutus and Harriet both looked up as if stung.

"What did you just say?" asked Harriet.

Dooley eyed her a little uncertainly, then gave me a questioning look. I shook my head. Cats usually don't like to be reminded they don't perform these feats of hanky panky in a vacuum. That there are other cats around who can hear everything that goes on in these unguarded moments.

"Um, that's what Max said you were doing down there," said Dooley, squarely dragging me into the thing. "So I just thought I'd ask…"

Brutus plastered a fake smile onto his face. "Yeah, um, the hanky panky. Well, it was a lot of fun, wasn't it, Harriet?"

"Actually we were not engaged in hanky panky," said Harriet.

"We weren't?" asked Brutus. Harriet was giving him warning signals for some reason, so he quickly amended his statement to, "No, we weren't."

"We were looking for clues," said Harriet. "Clues in connection to the case Odelia is working on. We figured if there's one body buried inside the wall of the basement, it stands to reason there must be others, especially as these two houses were inhabited by the same family once upon a time. Two basements, so why not two bodies, you know?"

I'd explained the whole story to Harriet, but it did strike me as peculiar that she would have known to look for dead bodies before she was apprised of the state of affairs. Almost as if she was psychic. Odd.

"And? Did you find any?" asked Dooley, and Harriet gave him a dirty look that was entirely undeserving for such an obvious question.

"No, Dooley, we did not find more dead bodies. And it is my firm belief that the basement, at least this one, is entirely body-free."

"Oh, that's great," said Dooley. "Odelia will be happy to hear that."

"So what about the mouse?" I asked, and this time Harriet's eyes flashed their anger at me. Why, I did not know.

"No, we didn't find the mouse. It probably got scared and ran off."

"Okay," I said. "So why were those gangsters yammering on and on about mice when Chase led them out of the house?"

"Oh, just tell them," said Brutus as he hunkered down on the couch, looking miserable.

"No, I will not tell them," said Harriet. "Remember what we agreed, Brutus."

"It's no use, Harriet," said Brutus. "They're too smart. They'll figure it out." He directed a quick glance at Dooley, then amended his statement. "Max is too smart. He'll figure it out."

"Figure what out?" I asked, intrigued.

"See? He doesn't have a clue," said Harriet. "So you better keep that big mouth shut, Brutus, or else—"

"Harriet got her head stuck in the wall," said Brutus. "One of the mice pretended to be our friend and lured her into its nest and then she got stuck. They're very devious, and they have no intention of leaving. Her name is Molly, by the way, and her partner is called Rupert, and between them they are the proud parents of an offspring of four hundred."

"Four hundred!" I cried. "That's a lot of mice."

"Tell me about it," said Brutus, shaking a tired head.

"If that's true Odelia will have to hire a professional. No way are we ever going to get four hundred mice out of the house."

"You're... not making fun of me, then?" asked Harriet after a pause which I used to think up ways and means to deal with these intruders.

"Make fun of you? Why would we make fun of you?" I asked, surprised.

She smiled. "I thought you'd have a big laugh at my expense when you heard I'd been fooled by Molly the Mouse and got my head stuck inside the wall."

"That could have happened to any one of us," I said, and I meant it. In fact it sounded like something that could very well have happened to me. "So are you going to tell Odelia? Give her the bad news?"

"Bad news about what?" asked Odelia as she joined us on the couch.

"Your basement is infested with mice," said Harriet. "And even though we tried to reason with them, they decided to stay put."

"Oh, that's fine," said Odelia with a wave of the hand. "They'll eventually move on."

"No, they won't," said Brutus. "There's four hundred of them, Odelia, and they have absolutely no intention of moving on. In fact they're going to stay where they are and try to drive us out of the house if they can manage."

"Four hundred," she said with an incredulous little laugh. "Phew. Are you sure?"

"We saw them," said Harriet. "And they're not nice mice either. They're devious."

Odelia held up her hands. "You know what? I can't deal with this right now. I'm still trying to wrap my head around this burglary. Good thing you guys caught those crooks."

"Good thing Chase was there to storm into that basement, guns blazing, saving you from financial ruin," I said.

She smiled as she petted me. "I wouldn't say he saved me from financial ruin, but he did save me from being burgled, which is a terrible feeling I never hope to experience again."

"Being saved, you mean?" asked Dooley, confused.

"Being burgled. People crawling all over your private space, and picking through your private stuff. It feels horrible, let me tell you."

"What's going to happen to those crooks now?" I asked.

"Oh, they'll be charged, and appear before the judge in the morning. I hope they'll go away for a long time. Did you say they fired off a shot?"

"Yes, to scare away the mice," said Brutus.

"And did it work?"

"It did,"' said Harriet. "Though now I wonder where they all ran off to."

Suddenly a piercing cry rent the air. It seemed to come from underneath us, and as we all ran down the stairs and into the basement, I saw that a sizable hole had been dug by the bullet one of the thugs had fired. Through the hole we could clearly see Marge, standing in her own basement next door, and screaming her head off.

The fact that she was surrounded by a swirling sea of rodents probably had something to do with that.

CHAPTER 23

*W*hen the commotion next door had died down a little, Marge decided to clear the table. No one was going to finish dinner now, and she liked to run a tight and especially a clean ship. And she'd just turned on the dishwasher and moved into the living room when she thought she heard a strange sound. Almost as if some animal was screaming up a storm in the basement. So she'd taken the broom and had pulled the little string that worked the light, and had moved down into the basement one step at a time. At first she didn't see a thing, but then, as she looked around, suddenly she saw that what she thought was the floor was actually a carpet consisting entirely of mice!

The carpet was undulating, and seemed to cover the whole basement floor!

And that's when she started screaming her head off.

"Mom!" Odelia called out.

Marge searched for the source of the sound, and saw that there was now a new hole in the basement wall, opposite the one where Boyd Baker's body had been found. This hole connected to Odelia's basement, and her daughter was saying something that she couldn't quite catch, as the mice were screeching up a violent storm at her feet.

So she added to the chorus and screamed some more.

Then two things happened: her mother came stomping down, carrying what looked like an old shotgun, and fired off a shot. The shot went wide and hit the wall, creating yet another hole.

"Mom! Stop shooting!" Marge yelled over the noise of the screeching mice.

And then her husband Tex followed in his mother-in-law's footsteps and when he saw the spectacle went a little white around the nostrils and said, "Oh, my Lord!"

"This is the first stage, Tex," said Mom. "See? It's always the rats that show the way. And they're showing us we need to build a bunker down here."

"It's not rats!" Marge yelled. "It's mice!"

"Same difference," said Mom. "Mice lead the way. Noah knew it, and so did Hitler."

What Hitler had to do with anything, Marge didn't know, but what she did know was that if someone didn't make these mice behave, she was going to freak out to such an extent it would be as if a nuclear bomb had exploded right then and there!

Tex, who'd disappeared, now returned carrying a spray can. He directed the nozzle at the mice and pressed the button. The smell of lavender filled the air.

"Is that my deodorant?" asked Marge.

"I didn't find anything else!"

"Mice love deodorant," said Mom. "Just look at those little buggers enjoying the heck out of that scent of lavender and pine."

Odelia, who'd made the trip through the hedge in record time, now also joined the party.

"I don't believe this," said Marge. "With four cats between

us you would think the house would be completely mouse-free, right?"

"The mice tricked them," said Odelia as she studied the horror scene with fascination.

"They did what?"

"Harriet and Brutus tried to reason with them and they tricked Harriet into sticking her head in one of their holes and she got stuck. She had her head stuck inside that wall all afternoon and part of the evening."

"Poor thing," said Mom.

"Poor thing! She should have killed that mouse, not try to reason with it!" Marge cried.

"Mice are God's creatures, too, and they have every right to live and thrive."

"They can live and thrive someplace else."

"So what do we do now?" asked Tex, whose bright idea of using deodorant on the mice had fizzled out. "How do we get rid of these critters in a humane and efficient way?"

"Humane, my ass!'" said Marge. "I want them out of here. Now!"

Four cats now descended on the scene: Max, Dooley, Harriet and Brutus, and stopped to stare at the seething mass of mouse.

"Why didn't the gunshot scare them off this time?" asked Brutus.

"They're quick learners," said Max. "They're probably used to gunshots already."

"Oh, dear," said Harriet. One of the mice said something that Marge couldn't understand and Harriet snapped, "I told you to beat it, and now look what you've done. They're going to massacre the whole lot of you, and it'll all be your fault!"

The mouse said something else that escaped Marge, and then Brutus said, "It's out of our paws now, Molly. I'm sorry. You brought this on yourself."

It all sounded very ominous, Marge thought, and when Mom raised her shotgun to check if there was another round in the chamber, the mouse called Molly seemed to make a plea.

"Yeah, that's a shotgun," said Harriet. "And you don't want to know what happens when that thing goes off and wipes out your entire family. It's going to be a bloodbath."

More pleading from the mouse, and finally Brutus said, "I know she missed that time, but that was just a warning shot. Next time she'll shoot to kill."

There seemed to be a lull in the proceedings, as the mice all gathered around the mouse called Molly and another, equally large mouse. Then the mice all looked up at Mom, their little noses twitching, and finally bowed their little heads. And before Marge's very eyes, the entire troupe suddenly moved off, like a military parade, towards the hole where Boyd Baker had been buried all these years, and moments later they'd cleared out and the basement was mouse-free once more.

No one spoke for a moment, then Harriet said, "I think we did it, Brutus. I think we scared them off."

"We did!" cried Brutus. "Can you imagine? They believed Gran would actually shoot them!"

"And you better believe it," said Mom, raising her shotgun, her finger itching on the trigger.

"No, Ma," said Marge, and quickly took the shotgun away from the old lady. "I can't believe we still have that thing," she muttered, directing a scornful look at her husband.

"It was in the tool shed," said Gran. "Kept it there all this time. It used to belong to my late husband," she explained for the sake of Odelia. "He brought it home from the war."

"The big war?" asked Tex.

"Hey, I'm not *that* old," she said, shooting an indignant glance at Marge's husband.

"Looks like they're gone now," said Tex, still holding on to his can of deodorant.

"And good riddance, too," said Marge.

"Well done, you guys," said Odelia, patting Harriet and Brutus on the head.

"See? I told you those cats would do their job sooner or later," said Mom.

"Let's go to bed, you guys," said Odelia, stifling a yawn. "It's been one hell of a day."

"It certainly has," said Tex as they all moved back up the stairs. Before following the others, Marge darted one final look around, just to make sure all the mice had gone, and that's when she saw that the hole Mom had made with the shotgun had revealed something stuck inside the wall. For a moment she feared it was another body, but when she moved closer she saw it was actually a small, leather-bound book. She lifted it out of its hiding place and saw that it was a diary, and that it was locked. Telling herself to give it to Odelia, she slipped it into the pocket of her apron, and promptly forgot all about it.

CHAPTER 24

The moment we'd long been waiting for had finally arrived: Odelia had told us that she was going to get more serious about dental hygiene and she hadn't been kidding. The reason for this was that recently I'd lost three teeth, due to the fact that they'd apparently outlived their usefulness. Yes, it happens, even to cats. And then Vena had advised Odelia to be more proactive in dental care and now there we were, the four of us filing into the bathroom to undergo our first ever session of having our teeth brushed.

It may surprise you to know this, but cats are incapable of brushing their own teeth. I know, for super creatures like us this is a strange state of affairs but there you have it. We need a human to do the brushing for us, unfortunately.

"What do you prefer?" asked Odelia. She was holding up two dangerous-looking devices. "Manual or electric?"

I hesitated. Tough choice. "Um… what's the difference?"

"Oh, Max, hurry up, will you?" said Harriet. "You're holding up the line."

"No, I just want to know what the difference is. How can I be expected to choose between two unknowns?"

"They're not unknowns," said Harriet. "One is manual and the other electric. How hard is it to grasp a simple concept?"

"Does it hurt?" asked Dooley. "It looks like it might hurt. Is it painful?"

"No, it doesn't hurt, Dooley," said Odelia. "In fact it's a very pleasant experience, provided you don't apply too much pressure on the gums."

"Yes, please don't apply pressure on my gums," he said. "My gums are very sensitive. I have very sensitive gums. Like, extremely sensitive."

"And how would you know?" said Brutus. "Have you ever tried brushing your teeth before?"

"Um, no," said Dooley as he licked his gums.

"Well, then? Just go ahead and do it already," said Harriet. "I don't have all night, you know. I have cats to see, places to visit."

"Try the electric one," I said. "That's probably the most modern, right?"

"Yes, it's important to be modern," Dooley agreed. "We're modern cats so we should have a modern way of brushing our teeth."

"All right," said Odelia, and applied a little bit of tooth-paste to the toothbrush, then approached me. I automatically recoiled. "Open your mouth, Max," she said. "Say aaah."

I said, "Are you sure it doesn't hurt?"

"Oh, we've been through this already," said Harriet. "Just do it already. Go, go, go!"

I rolled my eyes and opened my mouth a little.

"Wider," said Odelia. "Wider, Max."

"How hard can it be to open your mouth, Max?" asked Harriet, who was in one of her moods again.

"Just open as wide as you can," said Odelia. "That's it. Now who's a good boy?"

I don't like being talked to like a toddler, but I did as I was told and opened my mouth wide.

Now I want to add a minor PSA. Don't try this at home, folks. Most cats are not as well-behaved and well-trained as we are, and if you try to come anywhere near them with a toothbrush they'll bite you. And then they'll scratch you. And when they're done biting you and scratching you they'll punch you in the eyeball. And if you use an electric toothbrush they won't be happy that you're being 'modern' but they'll bite you even harder, because most cats don't like mechanical noises. But since this was Odelia, and I still had the recollection of having three teeth pulled by Vena, I was willing to give it a shot.

She lowered the toothbrush to my teeth and applied gentle pressure, then moved it all around.

"It's not so bad," I said, though the words probably didn't come out that clearly.

"What did you say, Max?" asked Dooley.

"I said it's not so bad!" I repeated.

"I didn't get that," said Brutus. "Did you get that, Harriet?"

"Who cares?" said Harriet. "As long as things are zipping along I'm happy. Just do the other side and be done with it, Odelia."

"Careful now," said Odelia. "I'm going to try massaging your gums a little."

Now that was too much. "It tickles!" I giggled, and promptly clamped down on the toothbrush. There was the sound of a crack, and when I opened my mouth again the thing had changed its tune. Instead of the nice humming sound it now produced a high-pitched whine. And then there was that odd smell. Like something burning. Yuck.

"Uh-oh," said Odelia.

"You broke it!" Harriet cried. "I don't believe this, Max—you broke the thing!"

"She's right," said Odelia, frowning at her electric toothbrush. "You bit down so hard you cracked the plastic."

"Oops," I said.

"Oh, well," said Dooley, suddenly sounding a lot happier. "Maybe next time."

"Don't worry, you guys" said Odelia. "I have plenty of other brushes." And she removed the one I'd broken and snapped another one on top of the device.

"Oh, shoot," Dooley muttered.

And so began a new chapter in our lives: from that moment on our snappers would always be squeaky clean, and plaque-free—whatever plaque is.

"Plaque is the enemy," Odelia explained. "We have to fight plaque."

"Great," I said as I grimaced. That toothpaste tasted horrible. "Can I go now?"

"Yes, you can," said Odelia, giving me a pat on the head. "You did good, Max. Next!"

Harriet, of course, was the next one to experience the miracle of the electric toothbrush, and before long she had a toothpaste smile, too.

"Plaque is the enemy," repeated Dooley reverently when it was his turn.

"That's right," said Odelia as she carefully applied brush to teeth and gums.

"And here I always thought dogs were the enemy," said Brutus. "Just goes to show you're never too old to learn new stuff."

Soon all of us had taken a turn on the hot seat and as we smacked our gums and tried very much to get the horrible taste of mint out of our mouths, Odelia put away the brush.

"Tomorrow, same time, same place," she said, sounding entirely too happy.

One thing I need to have a word with Odelia about,

though, is sharing stuff. I mean, when I passed by the bathroom later that night, I saw how Chase was brushing his teeth with the exact same brush Odelia had used on us. Now I know that humans think sharing is caring, but I, for one, would prefer my own dedicated toothbrush. After all, you never know where Chase's mouth has been, right?

And when he suddenly took the brush out of his mouth and stared at it, muttering something about a weird taste, then smelled it and grimaced, I could tell he was of the same opinion.

CHAPTER 25

*T*he next morning, bright and early, Odelia decided to drop by Courtyard Living, the landscaping company Boyd Baker used to work for. She'd discovered it was still in business, though now it probably belonged to the next generation of owners, or an entirely new one.

Courtyard Living was located in an old warehouse, where now a dozen small businesses were housed. She parked her car in the parking lot and got out. The warehouse used to be part of a candy factory, which had moved to another part of town fifteen years ago. She looked around. Someone was putting a display stand outside and carrying clay sculptures to place on top of it, and a wholesale clothes store was opening its doors, welcoming their first customers. It all looked very industrial chic and she liked it. Giving a new purpose to old factory buildings was a good thing. Better than to allow them to run down. She set foot for the landscaping place and as she walked in, several men dressed in green coveralls walked out, carrying gardening tools.

Once inside, she went in search of the owner, according to the website one Amabel Margarit. She found her in a cluttered office, her desk a big mess, papers covering every available surface, and a large whiteboard nailed to the wall with the weekly planning.

"Amabel Margarit?" she asked as she knocked politely. "My name is Odelia Poole, and I'm a reporter for the *Hampton Cove Gazette*."

"Oh, right, come on in. I have it here somewhere," said Amabel, rooting through the documents on her desk and shoving a snake plant that had seen better days out of the way. "Your boss called me last week and I told him I hadn't changed my mind—just hadn't gotten round to it yet. Ah, here it is." She produced a piece of paper, wiped off a few smudges of dirt, and proudly handed it to Odelia.

She then gave her a pleasant smile. Amabel was a sturdily built young woman, with dark hair and thick-rimmed glasses, and looked entirely too young to ever have known any member of the Baker family.

Odelia glanced at the piece of paper. It was the text for an ad in the *Gazette*, along with a picture of a garden, presumably one Courtyard Living had worked on.

"Um, I'm actually not here for this," she said, "but I'll take it, of course."

She looked up to see Amabel handing her a fifty-dollar bill. "Here. That should cover it, right?"

"Thanks. I'm actually looking into the murder of a man who used to work for you."

Amabel did a double take and placed her hands to her chest. "Oh, my god. Who?"

"His name is Boyd Baker, and he died fifty-five years ago. But at the time he worked for this company."

"Fifty-five years," said the woman, adjusting her glasses. "I'm twenty-eight, Miss Poole."

"I know. I just hoped you could point me in the right

direction. Names of people he worked with, maybe. Addresses. Something."

The young woman nodded. She darted a glance to a filing cabinet in a corner of the office. It was one of those old-fashioned sturdy metal things, that make a pleasant clunking sound when you slam the drawer home. She crouched down and opened the bottom drawer. "Now let me have a look-see. I took over Courtyard Living from my dad, who took over from his dad."

"I'd hoped as much," said Odelia gratefully.

"And any old personnel files my dad and granddad had, they kept in here. These days I keep everything in the computer, but if the old archive is still intact… Yes. Here we go. Boyd Baker." She took out the file as Odelia's heart made a little leap of excitement. She placed it on top of her desk and studied it for a moment. "So what do you want to know?"

"I'd like to know about his colleagues. Maybe some of them are still around."

"Fifty-five years…" She studied a pink card, covered in near illegible writing.

"His daughter told me he and his colleagues used to hang out at a bar after work. The Rusty Beaver? It's a flower shop now."

"Yeah, that name rings a bell. Our workers changed venues since the olden days, though. Now they hang out at the Brimming Beaker, which is just around the corner."

"Could I take a quick peek at Mr. Baker's personnel file?"

"Oh, sure. Be my guest," said Amabel, and handed her the file folder.

Odelia took a seat on the only chair that wasn't covered with objects, and leafed through the contents of the folder. There wasn't much of great significance there, as she'd feared. Boyd had started to work for Courtyard Living when he was eighteen, and had been an okay worker. And then, as she flipped a file that contained information about his paycheck, a scribbled note fell out. She picked it up and saw that it was some form of job assessment. In capital letters the words POLICE INTERVIEW had been written. It also contained a summary of the interview. Apparently Boyd had been accused by one of the company's customers of absconding with valuables belonging to the family where he'd done a job. And whoever had written these notes had added GET RID OF HIM? and underlined it three times.

She looked up. "Who is Mrs. Clifford?" she asked. "Aurelia Clifford?"

"The Cliffords were important clients of my grandfather and my dad, too," said Amabel, looking up from her computer. "Um, they used to live in one of those big mansions out on what is now called the Billionaire Mile. I don't think they still live there, though. Mrs. Clifford died many years ago, and her family got rid of the mansion."

Odelia studied the document a little longer, then tapped it with her index finger. "Any idea how I can get in touch with Mrs. Clifford's relatives?"

CHAPTER 26

*E*ven though we'd struck out the first time, Dooley and I were once again on our way to the macaw, in a second attempt to make her talk. And I mean this in the most benign way possible, of course.

"I can't believe Harriet and Brutus negotiated the mice retreat," I said as we walked along and soon found ourselves on familiar ground once more.

"Yeah, they did a great job," said Dooley.

"No, but I mean, it should have been us, Dooley, to create such a heroic moment, not Harriet and Brutus."

"Oh? And why is that?"

"Because we're the heroes."

"We are? I didn't even know this."

"Haven't you noticed how we always come up with the missing clue, that oh-so-important piece of evidence that nails the perpetrator? Or how we are the ones to save Odelia from harm?"

"I hadn't noticed, actually," he said after a moment's reflection. "I always thought we did this together. As a four-some, I mean. That it didn't matter who got the credit."

"Well, if you look at it that way…" Now I felt like a cad, of course. An egotistical cad. But Dooley was right. It didn't matter who got the credit, as long as whatever we were working on got resolved, whether it be chasing a colony of mice from the basement, or solving an old crime.

"I think Harriet and Brutus are very clever," said Dooley, rubbing it in some more.

"I think so, too," I said. "But are they clever enough?"

He gave me a strange look. "Max? You're acting a little weird."

I licked my lips. "It's because I don't feel I've done anything substantial on this case. We talked to one witness, and struck out, we didn't chase away the mice, and I can't even fit through the pet flap."

He smiled. "This is about the pet flap, isn't it?"

"I guess it is," I said with a sigh.

"You'll fit through the pet flap again, Max," he promised. "Just keep doing your daily exercises and before you know it you won't get stuck when you try to come and go."

His words warmed my heart. It was exactly what I needed to hear. "Thanks, Dooley," I said. "You're a true friend."

"And so are Harriet and Brutus," he reminded me, "and it doesn't matter who solves what crime, or who finds what clue. We're all in this together, Max, as a family. A team."

"Uh-huh," I said, a little shame-faced. Sometimes Dooley surprises me with his wisdom. And it's in moments like this that I am reminded that we should never judge a book by its cover. Dooley's cover might not be all that much to look at, but he has a big heart, and a keen intelligence when he decides to use it, and that's what matters.

We'd arrived in Morley Street, and we both took a deep breath.

"This is it, Dooley," I said. "We need to extract a confession now, you understand?"

"No, Max," he said. "We just need to have a chat with a friend, and if she tells us something important, great. And if not, also fine."

Damn, I thought as I stared at my friend. Who'd abducted Dooley and replaced him with Tony Robbins?

We moved between the houses and into the backyard and arrived at the same verandah we'd visited the day before.

Camilla was perched on the same spot, and when she saw us poking our heads through the window, she shouted, "Stranger danger! Stranger danger!"

"Hey, that's what I'm supposed to say," said Dooley.

"We're not strangers," I told the parrot. "We were here yesterday, remember?"

"Yes, we come in peace, good bird," said Dooley. "We're kindred spirits, all creatures of the Lord, and we wish you no harm whatsoever."

The bird eyed us with its head cocked to one side, but at least she'd stopped mimicking a fire alarm.

"Remember we asked you about a skeleton buried in the wall of our basement?" I said. "Well, we know his name now. Boyd Baker. And we also know when he died and how."

"Someone knocked him on the head and he didn't recover," said Dooley. "So they must have hit him pretty hard, and then they decided to bury him in the wall."

"This happened fifty-five years ago," I said. "So does that ring any bells? Any stories you might have heard about this guy?"

"Anything you can tell us will help us a great deal," said Dooley. "We want to bring the murderer to justice, because that is what we do."

"Yeah, well, the killer will probably be dead by now, but the relatives want closure," I said. "His son and daughter are still alive, and they've wondered all these years what happened to their dad."

Camilla was silent for a moment, then she spoke, and this time it wasn't to address Alexa and ask her how dangerous cats were. "I remember the Bakers," she said. "We used to live just down the street, and the Baker kids used to play with my family's kids."

"What was your family called?" I asked, wanting to get all the deets before she lapsed into silence again or, worse, turned foghorn on us.

"The Haddocks," she said. "This is a long time ago. I was a young macaw then, and had only just arrived in town. But the Haddocks treated me well, and even allowed me to fly around the house. The kids especially were very affectionate, and used to talk up a storm, asking me all kinds of questions. I loved it. I still see them from time to time, even though they gave me to their niece—my current human," she explained.

"Oh, so you don't live with these Haddocks anymore?"

"No, I don't. The kids grew up, and Mr. and Mrs. Haddock moved into an apartment and unfortunately couldn't keep me. And since the kids all live on the other side of the country, and one even overseas, they decided to give me to Laura Haddock. A wonderful person," she said warmly, "and I couldn't be happier."

"That's great," I said, genuinely happy for the parrot. "So... about Boyd Baker?"

"Boyd Baker was a horrible person. He used to yell at his wife all the time. Screaming and shouting. Flaming rows. There was even a rumor he was an alcoholic and came home reeking of liquor most nights."

"Is that a fact?" I said, giving Dooley a knowing look. "Rita Baker told our human that her father was a warm and loving man, and that her childhood was a happy one."

"I don't know about that," said Camilla. "All I know is that those were the stories I heard. And the number of times the police had to come and intervene were numerous."

"Uh-huh," I said. "So not such a happy home after all."

"No, not a happy home at all," the macaw said. "Or at least not in my recollection. Of course we all remember things differently, and you can't always believe everything you hear. Take the Haddocks for instance. Rumor had it Mr. Haddock liked to play with toy trains. But that wasn't true at all. He didn't even collect trains. What he did like were toy soldiers. You see? Toy soldiers, truth. Toy trains. Lie. Very easy to believe in the lie and dismiss the truth."

"Yes, well, I don't think there's such a big difference between toy soldiers and toy trains, though," I said.

The bird's eyes went wide. "Are you kidding me? There's a world of difference, and you wouldn't believe the number of times I intervened on Mr. Haddock's behalf and told the pets in our neighborhood the truth. But do you think they believed me? Of course not. Kept spreading foul lies. Especially the cats, of course, because cats are vicious."

"Excuse me," I said. "That's where you're mistaken. Cats are not vicious. In fact only last night a dear friend of ours negotiated a truce with an entire colony of mice and managed to get them to evacuate the premises, all without a single hair on their heads harmed. So don't you go spreading foul lies about cats, you hear?"

The bird was gloating, I could tell, but I couldn't stop. It's tough to have to listen to a bunch of lies.

"See?" she finally said. "I say one little thing and immediately you fly off the handle."

"I was just trying to set the record straight."

"And I was merely pointing out a few hard truths about your species and—"

"No, you weren't. You were spreading falsehoods, and I, for one—"

"You can't handle the truth, cat!" suddenly the parrot

shouted, and both Dooley and I were taken aback for a moment.

"Now look who's the violent one," I said.

"Oh, don't talk to me about violence," said the bird. "Violence is having your wings clipped just because some vet was given bad information at the university."

"Trouble with your vet, huh?" I said. "Trust me, I've been there. Do you know that last time I went to the vet she pulled three teeth? Three teeth!"

"Oh, three teeth is nothing," said the macaw, and lifted her wing then parted her feathers. "See those scars? That's where she stabbed me with a needle the other day. Allegedly so she could administer a vaccine, but we know better, don't we?"

"Oh, yes, we do. This vet kept poking me with so many needles I thought for a moment she'd mistaken me for a pincushion!"

The bird laughed heartily. "What's the name of your vet?"

"Vena Aleman."

"Mine, too!"

She stared at me, a smile on her face. "Well, maybe you were right. Maybe not all cats are vicious."

"It's the vets that are the vicious ones," I said.

"Too true," she said, and flew over to where we were sitting, and held up one foot. "Put it there, pals."

So I high-fived her, and so did Dooley.

"You should drop by more often," she said. "It's nice to shoot the breeze like this."

"Oh, sure," I said. "Next time we find the dead body of one of your old neighbors in the basement we'll be sure to tell you all about it."

She laughed, and so did Dooley and myself. And when moments later the bird's owner walked in, and saw her macaw fraternizing with no less than two cats, she yelled up such a storm I thought for a moment she had macaw blood herself.

CHAPTER 27

*W*hen Odelia entered the garage of Courtyard Living, she noticed that an older man who'd been sweeping the floor suddenly put down his broom and started walking away.

"Mr. Crocket?" she called out, her voice echoing in the large space. A flatbed truck used for gardening purposes stood parked in one of the garage bays, and large pallets stacked with bags of manure and mulch lined the far wall.

The man, if he'd heard her, didn't heed the call. Instead, he moved even quicker.

"Mr. Paddy Crocket!" she shouted, and broke into a jog. "Can I have a word with you please, sir?"

"Leave me alone!" the man growled, and had almost reached the large garage doors when he was momentarily waylaid by a truck entering the garage. It was all Odelia needed. By the time the truck had rumbled past, she'd already caught up with him.

"Hello, Mr. Crocket," she said. "My name is Odelia Poole and—"

"I know who you are," said the man. "I overheard you talking to the boss just now."

She wondered how he'd managed that, but then remembered hearing a noise when she'd been talking to Amabel. It must have been the man's silent footfall.

"I just want a quick word with you about Boyd Baker," she said as she fell into step beside him. "Amabel told me you've worked here the longest, and that you may remember Mr. Baker."

He had a distinct stoop, a ratty white beard, and a pockmarked face with shifty eyes but he was still pretty sprightly, trying to get away from her as fast as he could.

"I have nothing to say to you," he said.

"I just need some information about Mr. Baker. Did you know his body was found buried in my parents' basement yesterday?"

"Of course. I read your articles, Miss Poole. It was all over the garage this morning."

"Well, then you will also know that his relatives would very much like to know what exactly happened to Mr. Baker. All this time they thought he'd run out on them, while in fact he was right underneath their feet."

The man gave her a quick sideways glance. "Don't print my name in that newspaper of yours, Miss Poole. I don't want any trouble, you hear?"

"I won't print a word you tell me, or your name. Everything off the record."

He halted in his tracks. "Promise?"

"I promise."

He nodded curtly. "I remember Boyd. Nasty temper."

"Nasty? What do you mean?"

"I mean the man was a drunk and a bully. And a thief and a liar, if I'm going to spill my guts and spill it properly. He was involved in some kind of gang."

"A gang?" She remembered her grandmother's words about the kind of rumors swirling around about Boyd Baker. Gran had told Mom things used to disappear each time Boyd was on a job, and his personnel file seemed to confirm this.

"They stole stuff. Valuable stuff. Every time a member of that crew had a job at some place, stuff would mysteriously disappear, and a couple days later Boyd and the others would suddenly show up with a brand-new car, or some fancy new clothes or an expensive watch. It wasn't hard to put two and two together, Miss Poole."

"I saw in his personnel file that the police came here to talk to him."

"I remember. They figured he was the ringleader, but I don't think so. I think the real ringleader was Earl Paxton."

"Earl Paxton," she said as she jotted down the name.

"I wouldn't bother looking for him. He died a long time ago. After he was fired."

"And Boyd was part of his crew, you say?"

"Oh, yes, he was. Thick as thieves with Paxton, Boyd was. They used to hang out at the Rusty Beaver every night, talking big, and spending money like water. Back then the cops weren't as sophisticated as they are now, and it took them a while to catch on. But once they did, Paxton was arrested, and then Boyd suddenly disappeared."

"He was found with a diamond brooch on his person," said Odelia, and showed the older man a picture of the brooch.

He tapped it and smiled, showing a nice set of gleaming white dentures. "This is the kind of stuff they used to steal. Made a small fortune, too."

"And you were never involved?" she asked, quasi casually.

"No, I wasn't. I was too young and too fresh. They only trusted the people who'd worked here a while, and they didn't trust no outsiders. In fact when I said something about these accusations and rumors once, Boyd actually cut me." He stripped up his coverall sleeve and showed Odelia a tiny white stripe. "See? That's where he cut me. Happened fifty-something years ago but I remember it like it was yesterday. No, Miss Poole. Boyd Baker was a bad man, and if he was murdered he got exactly what he deserved."

❧

*C*hase had been going through the archives and gradually getting more and more covered in dust and spider webs. He cursed the genius who'd scrapped the budget to transfer all of these old files to digital format. So far he hadn't found anything useful, but he had a hunch, and over the years he'd learned better than to ignore those hunches of his.

There was more to this Boyd Baker case than met the eye, and he was determined to get to the bottom of it.

Dolores had asked him if he'd have put in so much effort if the body hadn't been found in what practically amounted to his own basement, and he'd told her that didn't matter one bit. A crime had been committed, however long ago, and justice needed to be served.

And then when she'd asked him if he'd have dug so deep if the body had dated back to the eighteen-hundreds, he'd told her there was no statute of limitations on murder, though he had to admit he might balk at investigating a crime that happened over a century ago.

But somehow, for some reason, this case intrigued him. A nice family guy like Boyd Baker, with a loving wife and two kids, cut down in his prime and suffering the indignation of being buried in his own basement. It just wasn't right, and he needed to find out how he'd died, and by whose hand.

And he'd been wiping a tickling dust bunny from his nose

when suddenly he struck gold. Or at least a report on Boyd Baker.

"Bingo," he said as he read through the report. It wasn't what he'd expected, though. All he'd wanted to find was the report on the man's disappearance and maybe the cop who'd handled the case at the time. If he or she were still alive he could have talked to them, asked if they'd had any leads back then. But instead he found a report filed *against* Boyd Baker. By the family of a Mrs. Clifford. For the theft of a brooch...

🐾

Odelia arrived at the offices of Mr. Clifford and announced herself to the receptionist. The young woman, though irked that Odelia hadn't had the foresight to make an appointment, still showed the kindness to talk to her boss and ask him if he could award a brief moment of his valuable time to a Miss Poole, journalist.

"About..." she said as she placed her hand on the receiver.

"Boyd Baker and Aurelia Clifford's brooch. He'll probably know what this is about," she added when the woman knitted her brows questioningly.

Five minutes later she was led into the office of Nate Clifford and offered the choice between coffee, tea or water. She picked coffee, and took a seat at the man's desk.

"I'm a little puzzled, I have to confess, Miss Poole," said Nate Clifford, who was a well-dressed man in his mid-thirties, wearing a power suit and a stylish haircut that must have set him back a considerable amount of money.

From what she'd been able to glean on the internet, Nate now ran the Clifford family trust, though what exactly this entailed was a little opaque. He seemed rich enough, so he probably either did a very good job, or received a very handsome fee for his services.

"I don't know if you know this, but Mrs. Aurelia Clifford filed a complaint against a Mr. Boyd Baker fifty-five years ago. For the theft of a brooch. Yesterday Mr. Baker was found immured in my parents' basement, and this brooch was found on his remains." She slid her phone across the desk and Nate leaned in to take a gander.

He frowned. "That's it," he said. "That's my great-grand-mama's brooch. See the inscription? AC/34? The AC stands for Aurelia Clifford and the 34 is the code given to this particular brooch. The Clifford family have always codified their items of value, so they could keep track—for insurance purposes. I'll be damned. And where did you find this, you say?"

Odelia told Nate the story of the missing Mr. Baker, and the police report that had been filed against him for stealing Mrs. Clifford's brooch. All this over half a century ago.

"Well, I'll be damned," Nate repeated, mussing up his nicely coiffed and gelled hair. "Do you know how much this brooch is worth, Miss Poole? Do you have any idea?"

"Um, I'm guessing a lot?"

"Try a hundred thousand," he said. "But actually it's price-less. This is a family heirloom. My great-grandmother received it as a gift from the Russian czar—they still had czars in Russia back then—and the idea was to bequeath it to her daughter, my grandmother, who loved the brooch and its history. But then one day it went poof."

"Do you know the story of its disappearance?" asked Odelia.

"Well, my great-grandmother died when I was a baby, but my grandmother talked about the brooch, for sure, and my parents. Apparently they'd hired a local landscaping company to spruce up the grounds, and when the job was done, the brooch was gone, too. Great-grandmama Aurelia always suspected the gardeners, and filed a complaint with the police. But of course nothing was ever found."

"So there's no question."

"None. This is the stolen brooch. Where is it now?"

"At the county medical examiner's office in Hauppauge," said Odelia.

"I'll get on the phone right away. This is a miracle, Miss Poole."

"It still doesn't explain how Mr. Baker got bricked up in my parents' basement, though," she said, "or how he got his head bashed in right before his immurement."

Nate smiled. "Well, I guess it's your job to find out, isn't it?"

❧

As Odelia walked out of the offices of the Clifford Family Trust, she almost bumped into Chase. They both laughed as he steadied her with a firm hand.

"We have to stop meeting like this," he said.

"Looks like you're on the same track I am," she said.

"I guess so." He took out his phone. "Look what I found." He showed her the official complaint Mrs. Clifford had made against Boyd Baker. "See the date?" he asked.

"Three days before he disappeared. Can't be a coincidence."

"No, it can't. What did Nate Clifford say?"

"He recognized the brooch. Positively identified it as belonging to his late great-grandmother and as the one that was stolen from her mansion fifty-five years ago."

"Well, I'll be damned," he said.

"That's what Nate said."

Chase raked his fingers through his long mane. "Do you think the old lady had something to do with the murder?"

"I doubt it. People like Aurelia Clifford don't go around bashing people's heads in. Besides, Boyd Baker was a large man, and she was old and frail. I think we can rule her out."

"A family member, maybe? Servant?"

"People like the Cliffords don't go around killing people."

"People like the Cliffords hire people who go around killing people."

"I don't know. I think what may have happened is that Boyd decided he didn't want to share the loot. I talked to Paddy Crocket, who worked for Courtyard Living, the landscaping company, when Boyd was there. He vividly remembers Boyd, and says he was a bully and a violent man, and part of a gang of workers who targeted the rich owners who hired Courtyard Living to maintain their gardens and grounds. The leader of the gang was a man called Earl Paxton. Now it's not that hard to imagine that Paxton and Boyd got into a fight over the brooch and Paxton got violent and bashed his associate's head in. And then, when he realized what he'd done, and knowing Mrs. Baker and the kids could arrive any moment, he buried Boyd in the most convenient place: the basement, and effectively wiped out the traces of his crime."

"It's a theory," Chase admitted. "Though I have to admit a very plausible one."

"Did my uncle have any luck with his part of the investigation?" she asked.

"What part of the investigation? He dumped the whole thing on my neck. Too busy writing enough traffic tickets to please the new mayor. Did you know we have quotas now? We need to write enough tickets or else we'll be demoted? Crazy politicians."

And as Odelia walked back to her car, and Chase entered the building, she saw she'd received a text from her mom.

'Cats are back from their visit to the parrot. Boyd Baker was not a nice person.'

Great. She'd already surmised as much herself, but it was always nice to get confirmation from an unsuspected source: the neighborhood parrot.

CHAPTER 28

*M*arge was at the library, extolling the virtues of the new John Grisham to one of her most loyal customers, when suddenly she remembered the diary she'd found the night before. It was probably nothing, but it could also be something. And hadn't close association with her daughter taught her to leave no stone unturned when investigating a crime?

So she dug through her purse and took out the mysterious diary. It was locked and she didn't have the key, but that wasn't going to stop her. Like a regular sleuth she took a penknife from the library kitchen and dug it into the lock, twisting until the clasp clicked open.

She felt ridiculously happy with herself and grinned like a kid. She was her brother's sister, after all, and her daughter's mother, though she didn't know if sleuthing talent traveled up and sideways and not down. She didn't care. She was going to make her own, however modest, contribution to the investigation. She flipped open the diary and frowned as she read the childish hand on the first page. The diary belonged to Rita Baker, twelve, and was filled with hearts and flowers and even pictures the girl must have cut out of the newspaper or magazines of that time. There was even a picture of James Dean, under which she'd written the words 'World's Biggest Dreamboat.'

Yeah, well, James had been a dreamboat, of course, thought Marge with a smile. She leafed through the diary, which was filled with the typical reflections of a twelve-year-old, about boys and her friends, and the teachers at school, the ones she hated and the ones she liked because they were generous with their grades. And then, suddenly, she discovered two pages that had been glued together. She stuck her trusty knife between the pages and carefully pried them loose. Time spent inside the musty basement had done its work and the pages soon became unstuck.

She frowned as she read the entry on the page—only a single paragraph but written in a very small but neat hand. She walked back to her desk and picked up her reading glasses. And as she read the entry twelve-year-old Rita Baker had written, an inadvertent gasp of shock escaped her, and then the diary was falling to the floor.

❦

*I*t didn't take us long to return from our errand, and when I saw that pet flap, I gritted my teeth.

"You can do it, Max," said Dooley. "You've been walking for miles. You lost ten pounds at least."

"At least," I agreed. All that walking to Morley Street and back must have sliced a couple of millimeters off my midsection. But was it enough to fit through that darn flap?

We would soon find out, for I was determined to win the fight with that recalcitrant flap.

"Maybe you should take a running leap," a voice spoke behind me. It belonged to Brutus, and he was dead serious.

"If you hit that thing with speed, you won't get stuck," he reasoned.

"Good tip, Brutus," I said. "And one I'm going to put into action right now."

"Maybe you should put some saliva on your fur," spoke another voice. It was Harriet, and she, too, had come to watch my near-Olympian attempt.

"Saliva?" I asked.

"Yeah, grease yourself up a little. Besides, if your fur is flattened against your skin it won't take up so much space."

"Duly noted," I said appreciatively. "All great ideas."

"See, Max?" said Dooley. "We need to work together as a team. As a family. As a band of brothers and sisters."

"Yes, Dooley," I said. "I get the message. And I'm very happy that you've all decided to bear witness to my attempt to beat the flap. But if you could please turn your backs to me now? I'm getting nervous from all the attention."

"You don't have to be nervous, Max," said Harriet. "We all want you to succeed. Isn't that right, you guys?"

Brutus and Dooley nodded seriously. "We're with you, buddy," said Brutus. "Wherever you go, we go, and if you want us to apply some of our own saliva to grease up that pudgy midsection, I will gladly make the donation."

This seemed a little too much, and I said so. I didn't need the saliva of all my friends on my precious bod. "I've got this," I said, as I gave a few tentative licks to my tummy.

"More, Max," said Harriet. "You can't sell yourself short now."

"Yeah, a lot more," Brutus agreed. "You need to really get in there and slather it on. Like the gladiators used to do."

"Did the gladiators use saliva before their fights?" asked Dooley, intrigued.

"Well, not saliva, maybe. They rubbed oil on themselves,

so other gladiators couldn't catch them. Oil makes you slippery, see, and then it's a lot harder to get caught."

"Maybe you should use oil, Max," Dooley said now.

"Or some other form of lubricant," Harriet added. "I hear duck fat is good."

"I'm not going to put duck fat on myself," I said, starting to get a little indignant.

"Just saying, Max," said Harriet. "If you want this, you have to do whatever it takes."

I stared at her. She was right. If I was going to do this, I needed to go all the way. "Okay," I said. "So where is this duck fat?"

My three friends all started chattering amongst themselves about where they could procure duck fat on such short notice, and finally Harriet had the solution. "I don't think Odelia stocks duck fat, but there's a tub of motor oil in the garden shed. I saw it there myself. Chase uses it to grease up the lawnmower, but I'll bet it'll do the trick just fine."

"Guck," I said, closing my eyes. But I'd told my friends I was fully on board with this endeavor, and I wasn't going to back out now, or show them I was a pussy, which of course I was, and not just in the literal sense either.

So we moved to the garden shed and walked in. And as Harriet had indicated, there was a nice big tub of motor oil waiting for me to apply a liberal helping to my corpus.

"Do you want us to do it?" asked Brutus. "Cause we will, isn't that right, you guys?"

"Of course," said Harriet, though she glanced at the black motor oil with a horrified expression. Her nice white paw would no longer be as pristinely white as it was now.

"I'll do it," said Dooley. "I'm gray, so no one will notice a few smudges."

"No, I should do it," said Brutus. "I'm black, so it will blend right in."

"I'll do it myself, thank you very much," I said, and after a short hesitation in which I had to overcome a certain hesitation, I stuck my paw into the black slurry and applied a nice helping to my blorange coat. It looked horrible, and it smelled even worse, but I had the support of my friends, so what could possibly go wrong?

"More," said Harriet when I paused after the first pawful. "You need to rub this stuff on your entire torso, Max, or it won't work."

I grimaced as I applied more of the gunk on my gorgeous fur. Yuck. But finally I was done, and wiped my paws on a patch of grass outside the garden shed. Then, accompanied by my friends, I walked back to the house. I stood there, poised and ready like an Olympian, as I stared down that flap.

"You're mine," I growled, psyching myself up. "I'm going to take you down, you flap."

And then I planted my paws firmly on the ground and took a running leap and then I was zooming—flying!—towards that pet flap like a chunky cruise missile.

And as I zipped in and zipped through, suddenly my progress was abruptly halted.

Yep. I was stuck again.

I had fought the flap and the flap had won.

CHAPTER 29

hen the doorbell jangled and Rita Baker saw Odelia Poole's face on her intercom, along with those of Detective Kingsley and Chief Lip, she knew this wasn't a social call.

For a moment, her heart sank, but then she decided to buck up and not postpone the inevitable. So she pressed the buzzer and opened the door.

Moments later, Odelia, Chase and the Chief walked into her modest but nicely furnished apartment. Odelia was the first to speak. "Rita, something has come to our attention so we decided to have a little chat, if that's all right with you."

She was friendly, Rita had to admit, and even the two cops were eyeing her with something akin to compassion, something that wasn't what she'd experienced before. It all brought her back to those stirring events fifty-five years ago, when her dad had gone missing, and the police had also dropped by. They hadn't been friendly then, practically accusing him of running off with the proceeds of the loot he stole from that woman.

She took a seat and invited the trio to join her. "Tea?" she asked, her voice slightly tremulous, but Odelia shook her head, then placed an object on the coffee table that she hadn't set eyes on since the night her dad had disappeared.

"Do you recognize this?" asked Odelia, who was taking the lead.

She nodded, and swallowed away a lump of uneasiness. So they knew.

"Yes, that's my old diary. Where did you find it?" She'd looked for that thing all over the place, and when she hadn't been able to find it her mom had vaguely thought she might have thrown it out with the trash.

"It was bricked inside the wall of my mother's basement, not that far from where your father was bricked in," said Odelia.

She nodded nervously. "Have you... read it?"

"Yes, we have, especially those glued-together pages."

She swallowed again. "Isn't there a law against reading other people's diaries?"

"I don't think so," said Chase. "But there is definitely a law against killing your father and burying him in your basement."

"I didn't kill my father," she said. "None of us did. It was an accident, I swear."

Odelia had picked up the diary. "My mom found it, and when she told me what you wrote in here I wasn't even surprised. Your father was not a nice man, was he, Rita?"

"No, he wasn't. He was horrible, and treated us like crap. Especially my mother."

"Did he beat her?"

She nodded, as tears trickled down her cheeks. "He almost killed her that night, and when we dragged him off her and he hit the edge of the kitchen table I knew he was dead before he hit the floor." She straightened. "And you know what? I'm not ashamed to admit it. My dad was a monster, and he deserved exactly what he got. So we thought it over, and decided unanimously to make sure his body was never found, and that the brooch he stole disappeared along with him, so people would come to the only logical conclusion: he'd sold the brooch and had run off with the money, never to be seen again. And good riddance, too."

"You told me you lived a happy life. That you had a warm and loving father. None of that was true, was it?"

"My father was a thief and a bully and a wife beater. He even raised his hand against me and my brother, but at twenty-one I wasn't prepared to take it anymore, and at sixteen neither was my brother. We made a pact. If he hit Mom one more time, we'd…"

"Kill him?" asked Chase.

"No, not kill him. But we'd make sure he never hit her again. We'd kick him out of the house and make Mom file for divorce, whether she liked it or not. So when Tom dragged him off Mom that night, and I shoved him, the combination of those movements made him hit his head. So basically, if you want to be accurate about it, we both killed him."

For a moment, no one spoke, then Odelia said, "I talked to a couple of people who knew your father back then. And they all agreed he was a pretty horrible person. In fact I haven't met anyone who had a kind word to say about him."

"We're returning the brooch to Nate Clifford, by the way," said Chase. "He's the great-grandson of Aurelia Clifford, the woman your father stole from."

"I know," she said. "I remember the story."

"You found the brooch on him?" asked Chief Lip.

"We did, but we figured we'd better bury it along with his body. It was the price to be paid for our freedom. For our mother's freedom."

"That brooch wasn't yours to bury, though," said Chase.

She nodded. "I know. And I'm sorry," she said softly. "But

if you compare the value of that brooch to the value of three lives, I'm not sure the brooch is worth more, are you?"

Odelia smiled. "We're not here to arrest you, Rita."

She looked up. "I don't understand. I just confessed that I killed my father."

"An accident," said Chase. "You said it yourself."

"I think the truth of what happened to Boyd Baker will probably never be fully known," said Odelia. "Though in the article I'm writing about the case I offer the suggestion that his associates and Boyd had a falling-out, and that they killed him in the struggle that ensued when they came to his house demanding he share the proceeds of the Clifford brooch sale. They killed him and in a panic buried him, never even going through his pockets and finding the brooch they'd made such a big fuss about."

She blinked. "You're not... going to arrest me? Or my brother?"

"No, we're not," said the Chief with a kindly smile. "I think you've suffered enough, Rita. You and your brother both, and your mother, of course."

"I think it's time to bury the dead past," said Odelia, "and that includes your father. And then you and your brother can finally be free."

"But... are you sure you can do this? Are you sure this is... legal?"

"We've discussed it," said Odelia.

"We held a family meeting just now," Chase explained.

"My mom and dad were there, and so was my grand-mother, and we all agreed."

"It may not strictly be lawful," said the Chief, "but under the circumstances I think it's the right thing to do. It is certainly in line with what my conscience is telling me to do."

"It's time to move on, Rita," said Odelia. "I know you as a warm, wonderful person, but I also know there's always been a darkness inside you. The secret you've carried all these years has eaten away at you, and now it's time for you to finally let go and heal."

As her three visitors got up and filed out of the apartment, she and Odelia hugged for a long time. The moment they were gone, she called her brother, and the first thing she said was, "It's over, Tom. It's finally over."

EPILOGUE

$\mathcal{T}$he Poole family was gathered once again in the Poole backyard, and this time there was even meat on the menu. The Pooles had recently become vegetarians for a brief while, but that hadn't lasted very long, and now Tex was flipping burgers again, and the sizzling meat spread its intoxicating aroma across the backyard and into the neighboring yards. Next to Marge and Tex live Marcie and Ted Trapper, who've been their neighbors since both families bought their respective houses. Marcie waved at us across the hedge, then disappeared into the house, while Ted sat with his feet in the tiny pool he'd installed a couple of summers ago. It was more a birdbath than a pool, but he didn't care.

"So that's it?" asked Gran. "The case is officially closed?"

"Yes, the investigation has been concluded," said Odelia. "And the conclusion is that we'll probably never know what happened to Boyd Baker, as all those involved have passed away by now, so crucial witnesses will never be able to tell their story."

"Some cold cases need to stay cold," said Uncle Alec as he raised a cold brewski.

"A toast," said Chase. "To Rita and Tom Baker, and the brave and selfless act they performed to protect their mom. An act that has hung like a shadow over their lives all this time, and now has finally been lifted."

"So have you decided what to do about the basement?" asked Uncle Alec with a twinkle in his eye.

Gran grumbled something under her breath that didn't sound very nice, and directed a searing glare at her son-in-law.

"We're turning it into a rehearsal space for Tex," said Marge.

"Yeah. We're going to put in a stage and a music installation," said Tex with the happy smile of a kid on Easter morning. "And when we have friends over I'll be able to entertain them without bothering the neighbors."

"If you didn't want to bother the neighbors you wouldn't take up singing," said Gran.

"So what about the nuclear holocaust?" asked Chase. "Aren't you going to prepare, Vesta?"

"Oh, I'm done with that nonsense," said Gran. "I read an article explaining how all this disaster stuff is just a bunch of hooey. Did you know that half the stuff they put on the YouTube or those social media is just a bunch of made-up baloney? Hard to imagine."

"Yeah, who knew?" said Uncle Alec with a grin.

"A second toast," said Chase now, as he held up his glass. "To Odelia, who had the courage to convince me and her uncle to drop the investigation into Rita and Tom Baker."

"It took some convincing," she said. "But it was worth it."

"Technically you broke the law," said Tex. "Didn't you, Alec?"

"Technically I have absolutely no idea what you're talking about, Tex."

"Boyd Baker?"

"I don't remember no Boyd Baker."

"The skeleton in the basement?"

"Never happened. And if it did, I'm sure no one is going to insist we drop all of our other work and focus on a fifty-five-year-old murder case."

"Does that other work include writing up tickets for every traffic violation within the town limits?" asked Tex, who wasn't happy that he'd recently been fined when he went to visit a patient, in spite of the fact he was a physician and had an MD license plate.

"You'll have to take that up with the new mayor, Tex."

"I'm taking it up with you, Alec."

"Are you trying to make me drop your ticket? That's against the law, Tex."

"I'm simply appealing to your sense of fairness, Alec. I have MD license plates."

"I could be persuaded to think about it, in exchange for another couple of sausages."

At the mention of the word sausage, all the adults in the backyard turned a little green. And as the conversation turned from murder laws to traffic laws to food safety laws, the four of us were seated on the porch swing and enjoying a lazy evening. Even though it was hot enough for Ted Trapper to sit with his feet in his birdbath, it was getting a little nippier, and soon summer would be over and autumn would roll in. Already it had been raining a lot, and there was a definite chill in the air.

"So how many pounds have you lost, Max?" asked Brutus now.

"Three, which is just enough to allow me free passage through the pet flap."

They all cheered for me, which frankly felt good. After my debacle with the motor oil, and Odelia having to use paper towels to get that junk off of me, I'd decided to get serious about my diet. So I'd been eating less, and I'd been taking regular walks around the block, and it had paid off. I was now slimmer than ever before, and I felt better, too.

"So how do you feel about this decision to let the Bakers off the hook?" asked Brutus.

"I think they did the right thing. It was an accident, and I don't think Rita and Tom should be punished for what were, in a sense, the crimes of their father."

"I think he's right," Harriet agreed. "And I, for one, think that Uncle Alec definitely made the right call."

"I agree," said Brutus.

Dooley was the only one who hadn't spoken. "So what do you think, Dooley?" asked Harriet.

"I'm not so sure," he said, much to my surprise. "I think Uncle Alec is making a big mistake. He should arrest Rita and Tom and punish them to the fullest extent of the law."

"Dooley?" I asked. "Are you feeling all right?"

My friend had a strange glint in his eyes. "Oh, I'm fine, Max. Absolutely fine." When we all stared at him, he suddenly burst into a giggle. "You should see your faces!"

"Is this supposed to be a joke?" asked Harriet.

"Yes, it is!" he cried, still giggling.

"Well, it's not funny."

His face fell. "Not funny?"

"Not funny at all."

"But... the documentary I saw on the Discovery Channel on stand-up comedy said that the trick to humor is to shock your audience. And hit them with your punchline."

"Whoever made that documentary obviously doesn't know the first thing about comedy," said Harriet, shaking her head.

"Not a clue," Brutus agreed.

"But, you guys! Gran asked me to be Tex's opening act once he launches his basement rehearsal space. She said I'm the best way to warm up the crowd for her son-in-law."

"Does Tex know about this?" I asked.

"No, Gran told me not to mention it to anyone. She wants to surprise him."

"Oh, he'll be surprised," said Harriet, and now she actually *was* laughing.

"Listen. I've prepared a couple of jokes," said Dooley, wetting his lips. "Um... a giraffe, a penguin and an elephant walk into a bar. Says the elephant to the giraffe, 'So how is the view from up there?' 'I guess not as good as the view from down there,' says the giraffe, and plucks the penguin from beneath his tush."

We were all silent, then I said, and I think I spoke for everyone, "Dooley, please don't become a comedian."

But Dooley wasn't going to be deterred. "I have to. For Tex. So how about this one? A priest, a nun and a basketball player walk into a bar. Asks the nun of the basketball player, 'How high do I have to jump to become a professional like you?'"

We all waited expectantly, but when nothing more seemed forthcoming, I asked, "So? What's the punchline?"

"I'm still working on it," said Dooley. "But how do you like it so far? Funny, right?"

We all groaned, and would have given Dooley a more thorough criticism if not suddenly the sound of our neighbor Marcie Trapper screaming caught our attention. And as I pricked up my ears, I could clearly hear the sound of four hundred mice clamoring.

Apparently Molly and Rupert had simply moved their colony into the Trappers' basement.

When we all looked to Harriet, now our official mouse

whisperer, she cried, "No way! I did it once but I'm not doing it again!"

Marcie kept on screaming, and soon the Pooles had all passed through the little gate in the hedge and were moving into the house next door, along with Ted, wet feet and all.

"Don't you think we should go over there?" asked Brutus. "We are cats, after all. We're supposed to take care of this mouse issue for our humans."

"I'm not going anywhere near them," said Harriet with a shiver. "Those mice are vicious."

"Oh, listen, you guys, I've got another one," said Dooley. "A mouse, a moose and a macaw walk into a bar."

"Okay," I said.

"That's all I've got. Hilarious, right?"

"Yeah, a real hoot, Dooley," I said.

There's probably a reason there are no famous cat comedians. We're not that funny.

Just then, Gran popped her head over the hedge and hissed, "Don't listen to those party poopers, Dooley. You're doing great. You'll have Tex's buddies rolling in the aisles. They'll keep coming back for more and more!" And then she disappeared again.

"See?" said Dooley. "Tex will be so happy with his surprise. So what do you call Prika's dad? Paprika. I can do this all night, so stop me if you've heard this one before."

I think that's the moment we all yelled, "Stop!"

EXCERPT FROM PURRFECT KILL
(THE MYSTERIES OF MAX 17)

Prologue

Chickie Hay was shaking her athletic frame to the beat, one eye on the floor-to-ceiling mirror, the other on the big screen where her choreo was being demonstrated by her personal choreographer Tracy Marbella. Chickie's next tour was coming up and she needed to get in shape, which is why she was working up a sweat practicing her moves and rehearsing the concert playlist until she had the songs and the dance routines down pat.

"Baby, baby," she sang, the music thumping through the room. She was wearing her usual pink leggings and her favorite pink sweatshirt—the same outfit she always wore when she started rehearsals. They were worn out by now, after years of use, but Chickie had a superstitious streak, and wouldn't wear anything except her lucky threads.

"Baby, baby, baby," she sang as she swung her hips and thrust out her arms.

She'd have preferred it if her trusty choreographer had been with her in person, to make those small corrections and improvements that make all the difference, but Tracy hadn't been able to make it. Doctor's appointment. No worries, though. Tracy always filmed her choreos and gave her clients plenty to work with.

"Baby, baby, baby, baby..."

Chickie frowned at her image in the mirror. Something wasn't right and she couldn't put her finger on it. Tracy would know. The experienced choreographer would only need a glimpse to know what was wrong and immediately correct her. 'No, Chickie—you need to relax those shoulders. And be light on your feet. Lighter! You look like an elephant stomping across the stage. Snappy movements. Snappy, snappy, snappy!'

And Chickie, even though she sometimes had a hard time following instructions, would do as she was told, because that's how much faith she put in Tracy's genius.

The fact of the matter was that she had a lot riding on the new album and the accompanying tour. It was her first one in five years, and already the media were calling it her come-back album. Then again, if you didn't put out something new every six months, you were already a has-been and ripe for a much-touted comeback.

She was proud of the new album. And felt that it was probably the best thing she'd ever done. She just hoped her fans, her Chickies, would like the new stuff. She'd invited a select few of them to the house the week before for a slumber party, so they could hear the new songs, and they'd loved them. Loved them! One or two had even fainted. Fainting was good. It was a sign she still had what it took to inspire her army of Chickies.

The sound of a pebble hitting the window had her look up in surprise. She walked over and looked out. It took another pebble to direct her attention to a tree whose branches reached the fence. One of her most fanatical

Chickies sat in the tree and was throwing rocks at her window. Oh, God. Not that guy again. But instead of indicating her displeasure, she gave him a little pinky wave. You had to keep the superfans happy.

She quickly moved back from the window before this self-declared #SuperChickie heaved a brick through the window and hit her smack in the face. Picking up her phone, she dialed Tyson's number, the man in charge of her small security crew.

"Yeah, Tyson. Olaf is back. He's sitting in a tree throwing rocks at my window. Can you get him out of there? Be nice about it—he may be nuts but he's still a fan. Thanks."

She shook her head in dismay. It was one thing to have fans but another to have crazies who followed you around wherever you went, trying to get a glimpse of you.

Trying to put the incident out of her mind, she resumed her rehearsal. One-step, two-step, pivot. One-step, two-step, pivot. Ouch. A sudden pain shot through her ankle.

"Oh, hell!" she cried, and threw up her hands. "Now see what you did, Olaf!"

And just as she picked up the phone to set up an appointment with her physiotherapist, the door swung open and she glanced up at the new arrival.

"Oh, hey," she said. "I think I twisted my ankle again. And it's all because of that horrible Olaf Poley. Can you believe he's actually throwing rocks at my window now?"

Suddenly two hands closed around her neck with surprising strength. She tried to fight back but to no avail. And as she started to lose consciousness, she remembered Tracy's words from their very first session: 'You need to work on your upper-body strength, missy! Train those noodles you call muscles until they're strong as iron bands!'

Oh, how she wished now she'd followed Tracy's advice.

Chapter One

I woke up from a strange sound. *Thump, thump, thump.* I could feel it in the pit of my stomach. As if some giant hand had grabbed the house and was shaking it all about.

And then I realized what it was.

"Earthquake!" I shouted as loud as I could. "Earthquake!"

And I was up and moving with great alacrity in the direction of the exit. I halted when a small inner voice told me I'd forgotten something. Something critical. I'd totally neglected to make sure my human was awake and responding to my cry of alarm.

So ignoring danger to life and limb, I turned back and checked on Odelia. Imagine my surprise when I saw that only Chase still occupied the bed, the covers pulled all the way up to his ears, blissfully sleeping the sleep of the dead in spite of my urgent plea.

"Earthquake!" I tooted in his ears. "Wake up, Chase—there's an earthquake!"

And to add credence to my words, I placed my paws on the burly copper and started massaging his mighty chest, not stinting on the odd claw extending from the odd paw.

"Not now, Max," Chase muttered, then turned to his other side and kept on sleeping.

"But Chase! You have to wake up! There's an earthquake and if you don't get up right now the house will fall on top of our heads!"

"That's nice," Chase muttered, even though I'm sure he couldn't possibly have understood what I'd just said. Chase is one of those humans who can't comprehend cats. Well, I guess most humans fall into that category. Only Odelia, Chase's girlfriend and my very own personal human, can speak to me, as well as her mother and grandmother.

My gaze briefly raked the spot where Odelia should have

been, and I reached out a tentative paw to touch the sheet. Still warm, so she must have gotten up just now. So why hadn't she alerted her boyfriend of the impending doom? Or me, for that matter?

And then, as I glanced around some more, I saw that there was one other individual missing from the picture: my best friend Dooley. I wasn't worried about him, though, as Dooley has the luxury of calling two homes his home, both Odelia's and her mom's, and had presumably opted to keep his own human next door company this particular night.

I decided to go in search of Odelia, as she seemed to be the only one who'd be able to rouse Chase from the land of slumber and into full wakefulness.

The loud noise that I'd identified as an earthquake had changed in pitch, and as I hurried out of the bedroom and into the corridor, suddenly I realized my mistake. It wasn't an earthquake but… music. Loud, thumping music. The kind that humans like to dance to.

Quickly putting two and two together I deduced that Odelia had gotten up early and was using these quiet moments before the dawn to perform some of that aerobics, as she calls it. She dresses up in fluorescent lycra and jumps around in sync with the music, watching other women donning similar attire do the same on her big TV screen.

So I waddled down the stairs, and the moment I arrived in the living room I discovered I'd been right on the money: there, jumping up and down and swinging her arms, was Odelia, dressed in pink, moving along to the beat of some very peculiar music.

And next to her sat Dooley, bobbing his head as if in approval of these proceedings.

I sidled up to him, after giving Odelia a once-over to determine if she was still of sound mind and body or had been bitten by some exotic bug and gone off her rocker. With humans you never know. They act sane and sensible one minute, and nuts the next.

"Have you been up long?" I asked as I hopped onto the couch and joined my friend.

"I woke up when Odelia got out of bed," said Dooley, who, judging from the way he was still bobbing his head to the beat, seemed to enjoy the extravaganza.

"I thought it was an earthquake," I intimated. "Until I realized it was Odelia."

"She's getting good at this aerobics thing, isn't she?" said Dooley proudly. "She's almost as good as those very lively ladies on TV."

Those lively ladies were kicking their legs so high into the air I winced, afraid something might give and they'd lose a limb or two.

"Yeah, she's improving with leaps and bounds," I agreed, though I still wasn't entirely sure whether the aerobics thing was good for her or detrimental to her health. "Why does she do it, though? I mean, what's the point of all this jumping and sweating?"

"She wants to get in shape," said Dooley, regurgitating the party line. Odelia had been talking about getting 'in' shape for weeks now, even though as far as I could tell she'd never been 'out' of shape. Odelia is a slim-limbed young woman with long blond hair and not an ounce of fat on her entire body. So why she would feel the need to put herself through this ordeal is frankly beyond me. But then I've never claimed to be the world's biggest expert on humans, and the peculiar species keeps confounding me every day.

"Next she'll want to run a marathon," I said.

"A marathon?" asked Dooley, as he smiled at the complicated movements Odelia was performing with gusto. "What's a marathon, Max?"

"It's where humans run for a really long time, like hours

and hours and hours, and then at the end, when they're almost dead, the first three people get a medal."

"They run…"

"And run and run and then they run some more."

"So what are they chasing?"

"Like I said, these medals."

"Are they edible medals?"

"I don't think so."

"Are they worth a great deal of money?"

"Well, yes, I guess. There's usually a gold medal, a silver one and a bronze one."

"Then that must be the reason. They run so they can get a medal and then sell it and use the money to buy food. Humans don't do these things without a good reason."

"Yeah, I guess they don't."

"Running just for the heck of it would be crazy."

"It sure would."

"Irrational."

We watched Odelia jump up and down some more, the music making the walls quake.

"So do you think Odelia gets a medal if she gets the routine just right?" asked Dooley.

"I doubt it. There's no medals in aerobics."

"Then why does she do it?"

"Um…"

We shared a look of apprehension. It had suddenly dawned on us that our human might be going crazy. Jumping up and down for no good reason at all. Odelia paused, and now clapped her hands, just like the women in the video. She turned to us, panting and wiping sweat from her brow with a towel. "What are you guys talking about?" she asked.

"I was wondering if you'll get a medal if you get your routine just right," said Dooley.

Odelia laughed. "Oh, Dooley. No, I won't get a medal. But

I'll feel really good when those endorphins start flooding my brain, and that's all the encouragement I need."

"She's doing it for the endorphins," said Dooley, sounding relieved that our human wasn't crazy. Then he turned to me. "What's an endorphin, Max? Is it like a dolphin?"

"I think so," I said. Though why Odelia needed dolphins in her brain I didn't know.

"Endorphins are hormones," said Odelia, now bending over and touching the floor with her hands. "When they flood your brain they make you feel happy. That's why they call them happy hormones. Plus, getting in shape makes my body happy and healthy. And you know what they say. *Mens sana in corpore sano*. Healthy body, healthy mind."

"Uh-huh," I said dubiously. "I thought it was an earthquake. So my body wasn't happy, and neither was my mind."

"I'm sorry, Max," she said. "But if I don't do this first thing in the morning I never get round to it. Is Chase up yet?"

"Almost. He was talking, but refused to get up when I told them about the earthquake."

"Best to let him sleep. He got home pretty late last night."

Chase had gone up to New York the night before, for a reunion with his ex-colleagues from the NYPD, the police force he'd worked for before moving to Hampton Cove.

"Chase should try napping," said Dooley. "It's very effective. Uncle Alec could put beds in the office so his officers can nap whenever they feel tired. Cats do it all the time."

"Great idea, Dooley," I said. "I love napping."

"And I'll bet it's great for those dolphins, too."

"I don't think my uncle will like the idea," said Odelia with a laugh. "But I'll tell him."

"Napping," said Dooley, "is the secret why cats are so vigorous, vivacious and vital."

On TV the routine had started up again, and moments later Odelia was jumping around again, the earthquake moving up on the Richter scale. To such an extent that moments later Chase came stomping down the stairs, rubbing his eyes and yawning widely. He stood watching Odelia while she tried to kick and touch the ceiling, then shook his head and moved into the kitchen to start up his precious coffeemaker.

Soon the sounds of Odelia's aerobics routine mingled nicely with Chase's baritone voice singing along. And as he rubbed his stubbled jaw and then stretched, a third person entered the fray: it was Marge, Odelia's mom, and she looked a little frazzled.

Odelia pressed pause on the remote, and stood, hands on knees, panting freely.

"Odelia, honey, I need your help," said Marge as she took a seat on the couch.

"Sure, anything," said Odelia, grabbing for her towel again.

"It's your grandmother."

Odelia closed her eyes and groaned. "What has she gone and done now?"

"You know how she agreed to sing backing vocals in your father's band? Well, she's just announced she's tired of playing second fiddle and she's starting a solo career."

"Of course she has," said Odelia as she toweled off and sat down next to her mother.

"She wants to be the next Beyoncé," said Marge.

"Beyoncé?" said Odelia with a laugh. "But... Gran can't even sing."

"Not to mention she's old enough to be Beyoncé's grandmother."

"Who's Beyoncé?" asked Dooley.

"A famous singer," I said. "And a very popular one, too."

"She's been nagging me to get her a singing coach," said Marge, "and just now she told me she wants me to find her a manager—one of those power managers that can launch her career straight into the stratosphere, on account of the fact that she doesn't have time to build it up slowly."

"And what did you tell her?"

Marge threw up her arms. "That I don't know the first thing about showbiz or power managers or singing coaches! And that if she wants to be the next Beyoncé maybe she should start by joining a singing competition. They'll be sure to tell her if she's any good."

"Good advice," said Chase, who was sipping from a cup of coffee and looking a little bleary-eyed. "The best way to knock some sense into your grandmother is to subject her to a nice round of criticism—just as long as it's not us who provide the criticism I'm sure she'll take it on the chin and move on to her next foolish whim."

"I sincerely hope that's all this is," said Marge. "With a husband in showbiz, and now an elderly parent, life is starting to get a little too showbizzy to my liking. Not only is Tex expecting me to go to every single one of his performances and cheer him on, soon Mom will expect me to go to all of her performances, too. And here I thought things slowed down once the kids were out of the house. Looks like things are just getting started!"

"Well, trust me, Mom," said Odelia as she patted her mother's arm. "I don't have any plans to go into show business, so there's that. And I'm sure Gran's ambitions will be as short-lived as most of her endeavors. I give it a month —tops."

"Speak of the devil," Chase muttered through half-closed lips.

Gran had just walked in, looking as sprightly and vivacious as ever. "Odelia!" she cried as she made a beeline for her granddaughter. "You're up. Good. Look, I need you to be honest with me. Do you think I've got what it takes to be the next Beyoncé?"

"Um... I don't know, Gran," said Odelia, treading carefully.

'Maybe you can sing something for us?" Chase suggested. "How about *Single Ladies?*"

Gran eyed Chase strangely. "Single ladies? You don't have to rub it in, young man. It's true I'm a single lady right now but it's not very nice of you to point that out. Very rude."

"No, that's the name of the song," said Chase. "*Single Ladies.*"

"Never heard of it," said Gran, still giving Chase a nasty look.

"Okay. So how about *Crazy in Love?*"

"I'm not, but thanks for the suggestion. I'll sing Beyoncé's biggest hit, shall I?" She took a deep breath, then placed her hands on her chest and closed her eyes. *"Some boys kiss me, some boys hug me, I think they're oka-ay,"* she bleated in a croaky voice.

"Gran?" said Odelia, interrupting the songbird. "That's Madonna, not Beyoncé."

"Shut up and let me sing. *Cause we're li-ving in a mate-rial world...*"

It sounded a little awful, I thought, and judging from the frozen looks on the faces of all those present I wasn't alone in my assessment. Finally, Gran finished the song and opened her arms in anticipation of the roaring applause she clearly felt she deserved. When the applause didn't come, she eyed us with annoyance.

"Well? What do you think?" she snapped.

"Um... not bad," said Odelia. "Not bad at all. But you know that's not Beyoncé, right?"

"'Of course it's Beyoncé. One of the woman's greatest

hits. So how about you, Marge? What do you reckon? Knocked it out of the park, huh? Hit a home run?"

"Um...." said Marge, darting anxious glances at her daughter.

"Blown away," said Gran with a nod of satisfaction. "That's what I was going for. Chase?"

"Loved it," Chase lied smoothly. "Best Beyoncé imitation I've ever heard."

"Perhaps you should put a little more pep in your show, though," said Marge.

"Oh, you'll get all the pep you need. I've asked Beyoncé's choreographer to work with me and he graciously accepted. In fact we're starting rehearsals today."

"Beyoncé's choreographer is going to work with you?" asked Odelia.

"Sure. You all know him. My ex-boyfriend Dick Bernstein. He's worked with Beyoncé for years. Choreographed all of her big shows, here and overseas. I asked him and he immediately said yes. It's gonna be a smash, you guys. And now if you'll excuse me—I gotta get ready before Dick arrives. Oh, and Marge? Can you tell Tex I'm not coming in today? My career takes precedence over that silly receptionist business. Toodle-oo!"

And with these words she was off, leaving us all stunned.

Except for Dooley, who was still wondering, "So who's Beyoncé?"

Chapter Two

Odelia was just about to walk into her office, after dutifully informing her father that Gran wouldn't be coming in today because she needed to launch her career, when a loud honking sound waylaid her. She looked up and saw that her uncle was trying to catch her attention.

Walking over to his squad car, she greeted him with a smile and a chipper, "Hey, Uncle Alec. I was just about to call you about the council's new fuel emission rules."

But Alec looked grim. He tapped the side of the door. "Get in, Odelia."

"Why? What happened?"

"You better sit down for this."

With a puzzled frown, she got in and slammed the door closed. "What's going on?"

"Do you know this lady?" he asked, gesturing to the radio, where a song of Chickie Hay was playing.

"Sure. Who doesn't? She's only one of the most famous pop stars of the last decade."

"Well, now she's one of the most famous dead pop stars of the last decade," he said with a set look.

Odelia did a double take. "Chickie Hay died?"

"This morning. Her housekeeper found her. Strangled."

"Strangled!"

Uncle Alec nodded, tapping his fingers on the steering wheel. "I called Chase and he's going to meet us there. I want you on this one, Odelia, cause I have a feeling it's not going to be one of our easiest cases. And since she is what you just said she is, there's going to be a lot of scrutiny and a lot of pressure, you understand?"

Odelia nodded, still stunned by the terrible news. "Strangled," she repeated softly.

"Yeah, what a shame, right? I actually liked her music."

He stomped on the accelerator and the car peeled away from the curb. Soon they were zooming along the road. Odelia picked out her phone and decided to call her editor first. She had a feeling he wouldn't mind if she didn't show up for work, as long as she landed him the big scoop on who the murderer of Chickie Hay could possibly be.

"Maybe pick up your cats?" Uncle Alec suggested. "It's all paws on deck for this one."

She nodded as she waited for her call to connect.

Moments later she was back at the house, and she hopped out. "Yeah, hey, Dan. There's been a murder. Yeah, Chickie Hay. I'm heading over there now with my uncle." She opened the front door and yelled, "Max, Dooley, Harriet, Brutus! Got a job for you!"

As expected, Dan was over the moon, not exactly the kind of response a feeling fan or loving relative would like to see, but understandable from one who sells papers for a living.

Four cats came tripping into the hallway, all looking up at her expectantly. She crouched down. "There's been a murder," she said, without preamble, "and I need your help. Are you up for it?" They all nodded staunchly, and she smiled, doling out pets for her four pets. "Come on, then," she said. "Uncle Alec is taking us over there now."

Four cats hopped into the back of the pickup, and then they were mobile again, en route to Chickie Hay's no doubt humble abode.

The house was located in Hampton Cove itself, and not near the beach as most of these celebrity homes usually were. It wasn't a manor either, but a house that sat hidden behind a fence atop a modest hill. The only thing indicating this was no ordinary home was the gate you had to pass through. Uncle Alec pressed the intercom with a pudgy finger and held up his badge. The gate swung open and Odelia saw that the drive angled steeply up. Moments later they were surrounded by a perfectly manicured garden, and soon the car crested the hill and the house appeared. It was a large structure, painted a pastel pink and looking modern and cozy at the same time. Chase stood waiting for them, leaning against his pickup, and pushed himself off the hood when he saw them.

"Bad business," he said, giving Alec a clap on the shoulder and Odelia a quick kiss.

The four cats exited the car, then disappeared from view to do what they did best: interviewing pet witnesses and scoping out the place from their own, unique angle.

"Where is she?" asked Uncle Alec.

"Upstairs," said Chase, gesturing with his head to a large plate-glass window right over their heads. "She was rehearsing for her upcoming tour when it happened."

"No one saw anything?"

"I only got here five minutes ago so I figured I'd wait for you guys."

The woman who greeted them at the door was red-faced and very emotional. Judging from the way she was dressed she was perhaps the housekeeper who'd found Chickie, Odelia thought, and when she asked her the question, the woman nodded affirmatively.

"Yes, I found Miss Hay," she said. She was short and round, with a kind face and a lot of curly brown hair piled on top of her head. Her name was Hortense Harvey.

"Please show us," said Uncle Alec, adopting a fatherly tone.

"Did anyone come near the body?" asked Chase. When the woman uttered a quiet sob, he quickly apologized and corrected himself. "Did anyone come near Miss Hay?"

"No, detective. You told me over the phone not to allow anyone in so I locked the door—well, me and Tyson Wanicki, Miss Hay's bodyguard."

"Where was Mr. Wanicki when this happened?" asked Odelia.

"You will have to ask him yourself, I'm afraid," said Hortense. "I haven't been able to talk to anyone about what happened. I've been upstairs in my room crying."

Odelia decided to postpone the questions for later, when

they had a chance to properly sit down with the woman. For now they needed to see what had happened.

Hortense led them up a staircase and into the upstairs hallway, then to the last door on the left, where a large man stood sentry. When they arrived, he nodded. With his bald pate, horn-rimmed glasses and white walrus mustache he looked more like a kindly uncle than a hardened security man. He definitely did not look like Kevin Costner.

The bodyguard answered in the affirmative when Uncle Alec asked if he was Tyson, and stepped aside so the trio could enter the room. It was a large room, one wall consisting of a giant mirror, not unlike the workout rooms in fitness clubs. Speakers were still blaring and on a giant screen a woman was going through some dance moves.

"You told me not to touch a thing so I didn't touch a thing," said Tyson. He darted a sad look at the lifeless body in front of the mirror, and a lone tear stole from his eye.

Uncle Alec placed an arm around his broad shoulders. "You better get out of here, Mr. Wanicki. But don't go too far. We want to have a word with you."

"Yes, Chief," said the man deferentially as he swiped at his teary face.

At the door, Hortense still stood, reluctant to enter. "You, too, Miss Harvey," said Alec.

"Yes, Chief Lip," said the woman, and the Chief closed the door behind them.

Once they were alone, he crouched down next to the body of the singer, shaking his head in dismay. "What a waste," he muttered.

Odelia's sneakered feet made a squeaking sound as she crossed the floor. The first thing that struck her was how small Chickie Hay looked. She also noticed the bruising on the famous singer's neck and the bulging eyes, a clear indication of how she'd died.

"You a fan?" asked Chase.

"Not a big fan, but I like her music, yeah," said Odelia.

"Me, too," said Chase, a little surprisingly. He was strictly a country and western guy, but then again, Chickie Hay had country roots, and her first albums had been all country.

Odelia glanced up at the video screen where the choreographer still stood showcasing complicated and exhausting-looking moves, and Odelia remembered she'd been going through a similar routine herself only an hour before.

"Abe will be here soon," said Uncle Alec, "but if you want you can start the interviews now. No sense in all of us waiting around for the big guy to show up, right?"

After one last look at Chickie, Odelia and Chase filed out of the room and saw that the bodyguard and the house-keeper had decided to wait outside. And as Hortense led them to a room where they could set up the interviews, Odelia wondered if Chickie had pets for her cats to interview. She hoped so, and she hoped they'd seen what had happened to their mistress.

Chapter Three

I actually felt like the leader of the pack for once, as I moved along the greenery in the direction of the back of the house, three cats following my lead. It didn't last long, though, for soon Harriet fell into step beside me, scanning the grounds with her sharp eyes. "Our objective is to locate and interrogate any pets on the premises, Max," she said, then darted a stern-faced look over her shoulder at the others. "And that goes for you two, too. Keep your eyes peeled, boys—remember, Odelia is counting on us."

I heaved a deep sigh as she overtook me and then moved ahead of me, Brutus hurrying to keep up with her. Dooley and I fell behind and then lost sight of them.

"What is it, Max?" asked Dooley. "Why are you looking so sad all of a sudden?"

"For once I wish I were the one in charge—me being Odelia's cat and all."

"But you are the one in charge, Max."

"Tell that to Harriet. I'm sure she doesn't see it that way."

He gave me a reassuring smile. "To me you'll always be the one in charge, Max."

I have to tell you I was touched. It was one of the nicest things anyone has ever said to me. "Thanks, Dooley," I said. "That's very sweet of you to say."

"So what do we hope to find here, Max?"

"No idea. But you know what these ultra-rich celebrities are like. They like to keep some special pets no one else has. So we might expect a pet boa constrictor, a pet llama, a pet chimpanzee—anything goes."

"Got it," he said, looking appropriately serious for this most important mission.

"What do you think about Gran becoming the next Beyoncé?" I asked as we roamed around Chickie Hay's gorgeous garden, exotic plants covering every available surface.

"I'm not sure," he said. "You still haven't told me who this Beyoncé person is."

"Oh, right. Well, Beyoncé is—"

But unfortunately I was interrupted by the call of a bird. One glance told me it was a big bird—in fact a large peacock. And Harriet was already engaging it in conversation.

I resumed my instructive moment with Dooley. "So Beyoncé is—"

"What are you doing here?" asked a gruff voice in our immediate vicinity.

I glanced over and found myself locking eyes with a tiny French Bulldog.

"Oh, hi," I said. "My name is Max and this is Dooley, and we're here to—"

"Trespass, that's what you're doing," he barked. "Get lost, cats. This is private property."

"But—"

"No buts. Get lost now or I'm calling security."

"Oh," said Dooley. "I thought you were security, tiny dog."

The dog's expression darkened. "What did you just call me?"

"Um? Security?"

"No, the other thing. Starts with a T and ends with Y. Horrible slur."

"Tiny dog?"

"That's the one. I'm going to have to punish you for that. Lie down and willingly submit to your punishment, cat. Come on, now. I'm going to give you one nip in the butt. And if you repeat the slur I'll have to give you two nips, so don't go there."

"But, tiny dog," said Dooley, "we're simply here because—"

"And you just had to go there, didn't you? Lie down and accept two nips in the butt." And he approached Dooley to administer the appropriate punishment.

But Dooley wasn't taking it lying down. He wasn't even taking it standing up. Instead, he said, "But, tiny dog, all we want is to—"

"And there you go again. Three nips is the proper punishment and you will take it like a cat, cat. Now face the other way. This will only take a second, and it will remind you not to repeat these horrible slurs to my freckled face."

"Look, tiny dog..." Dooley began.

"Four is the score! You're not the smartest cat in the litter, are you, cat? Four nips in the butt."

"Look, we're here to investigate the murder of Chickie

Hay," I said. "So if you could tell us what you know we would be very much obli—"

"Murder?" asked the dog, expression darkening. "What are you talking about, cat?"

"Our human is a detective," I explained, "and she was called here to investigate the murder of Miss Hay. And as her pet sleuths we were hoping you could shed some light on the matter."

"This is crazy," said the doggie. "Chickie Hay is my human, and she's not dead. She's alive and kicking. Well, maybe not kicking, exactly, but singing and dancing. In fact she's right up there practicing for her new tour. And if you don't believe me just direct your attention yonder and you'll hear her angelic voice belting out her latest hit song."

We directed our attention yonder, as instructed, but I couldn't hear anyone belting out any song, new or old. In fact I didn't hear a thing, except for Harriet yapping a mile a minute to the peacock, who was looking slightly dazed from all this verbal diarrhea.

"Um? I don't hear anything," Dooley finally announced.

"Me neither," I said. "Are you sure she's up there?"

"Of course I'm sure," said the doggie, even though he now looked slightly worried.

The French Bulldog stared at us, clearly distraught, then, suddenly and without another word about nips in the butt, tripped off in the direction of the house.

"Not much of a witness," said Dooley. "He doesn't even know his human is dead."

"He could still prove a valuable witness," I said.

"He could?"

"He might not know what he knows and when we talk to him again, he might remember what it is that he didn't know he knew. If you know what I mean."

Dooley stared at me. "I'm not sure I got all that, Max."

I wasn't sure I got it myself. That's the trouble with being a detective: you just muck about for a while, hunting down clues, speaking to pets and people, and finally you may or may not happen upon a clue that may or may not be vital to the investigation. And if you're lucky you end up figuring out what happened. And if you're unlucky, well, then Harriet beats you to it by extracting the telling clue from a silly-looking big bird with spectacular plumage.

ABOUT NIC

Nic Saint is the pen name for writing couple Nick and Nicole Saint. They've penned novels in the romance, cat sleuth, middle grade, suspense, comedy and cozy mystery genres. Nicole has a background in accounting and Nick in political science and before being struck by the writing bug the Saints worked odd jobs around the world (including massage therapist in Mexico, gardener in Italy, restaurant manager in India, and Berlitz teacher in Belgium).

When they're not writing they enjoy Christmas-themed Hallmark movies (whether it's Christmas or not), all manner of pastry, comic books, a daily dose of yoga (to limber up those limbs), and spoiling their big red tomcat Tommy.

www.nicsaint.com

The Mysteries of Max

Purrfect Murder

Purrfectly Deadly

Purrfect Revenge

Box Set 1 (Books 1-3)

Purrfect Heat

Purrfect Crime

Purrfect Rivalry

Box Set 2 (Books 4-6)

Purrfect Peril

Purrfect Secret

Purrfect Alibi

Box Set 3 (Books 7-9)

Purrfect Obsession

Purrfect Betrayal

Purrfectly Clueless

Box Set 4 (Books 10-12)

Purrfectly Royal

Purrfect Cut

Purrfect Trap

Purrfectly Hidden

Purrfect Kill

Purrfect Santa

Purrfectly Flealess

Nora Steel

Murder Retreat

The Kellys

Murder Motel

Death in Suburbia

Emily Stone

Murder at the Art Class

Washington & Jefferson

First Shot

Alice Whitehouse

Spooky Times

Spooky Trills

Spooky End

Spooky Spells

Ghosts of London

Between a Ghost and a Spooky Place

Public Ghost Number One

Ghost Save the Queen

Box Set 1 (Books 1-3)

A Tale of Two Harrys

Ghost of Girlband Past

Ghostlier Things

Charleneland

Deadly Ride

Final Ride

Neighborhood Witch Committee

Witchy Start

Witchy Worries

Witchy Wishes

Saffron Diffley

Crime and Retribution

Vice and Verdict

Felonies and Penalties (Saffron Diffley Short 1)

The B-Team

Once Upon a Spy

Tate-à-Tate

Enemy of the Tates

Ghosts vs. Spies

The Ghost Who Came in from the Cold

Witchy Fingers

Witchy Trouble

Witchy Hexations

Witchy Possessions

Witchy Riches

Box Set 1 (Books 1-4)

The Mysteries of Bell & Whitehouse

One Spoonful of Trouble

Two Scoops of Murder

Three Shots of Disaster

Box Set 1 (Books 1-3)

A Twist of Wraith

A Touch of Ghost

A Clash of Spooks

Box Set 2 (Books 4-6)

The Stuffing of Nightmares

A Breath of Dead Air

An Act of Hodd

Box Set 3 (Books 7-9)

A Game of Dons

Standalone Novels

When in Bruges

The Whiskered Spy

ThrillFix

Homejacking

The Eighth Billionaire

The Wrong Woman

Printed in Great Britain
by Amazon